I0549542

CROAKIES & SCREAM

SAM CHEEVER

ELECTRIC PROSE PUBLICATIONS

Magical chaos, old enemies, new adversaries, and danger around every corner...I HATE this time of year!

Okay, I'll admit it, this is my least favorite time of year. Yeah, I understand the enchantment of the season...I get that...but most people don't have jobs that involve wrangling magic. During the last three months of the year, magical influences run rampant. And that means a lot more work for me.

And this year is the worst of all.

Why you ask?

Because I'm not only trying to wrangle the out-of-control magic artifacts flying around all over the place. This year, I also have to try to keep a magical cat and a talking frog out of trouble.

Goddess take the wheel.

Things are about to get really ugly.

1

DANG THE SUCKY PARTS!

"Watch out!"

I ducked just in time to keep from getting hit by Nurse Ratchet's bedpan. The nasty curve of dented and pocked metal shot past where my head had been and clanged into the wall, clattering down onto my sales counter. Behind me, Sebille leaped over the magical vacuum cleaner currently trying to suck up Mr. Slimy, and smacked the bedpan down as it tried to rise again.

I grabbed the frog, giving him a smile that I hoped would help his eyes sink back into his head before they popped out, and hurried over to dump him into his fish tank for protection.

"Incoming!" Rustin's voice shouted

I turned to find Blackbeard's sword skimming through the air, SB the parrot riding its hilt and painting the air around him blue.

I ducked sideways as the sword slashed toward my heart and reached out, clasping the hilt and sending SB into the air on another wave of foul language overlaid by bleeps.

The parrot dropped onto my shoulder among a cloud of feathers, huffing out a breath as I fell backward, my knees finally giving out on me.

"Avast ye, Lass. Tis the bleepin' devil's spawn stirrin' the bubblin' cauldron this eve. We'll be blessed ta find the bleepin' back end of the moon without losin' our bloody tail feathers to a bleepin' magical trickster."

I sucked air, watching as Rustin wrangled a golden theater mask that kept trying to fix itself onto his ghostly face. I knew I should go help him, but I needed a minute to gather my breath and count all my fingers and toes.

"Time check!" I yelled, praying the response would be the right one. It had been a long eight hours, and I didn't know how much energy I still had in me.

The mask thwucked onto Rustin's face, sending him reeling back to smack against a bookshelf. The impact sent several magical volumes tumbling to the floor.

The vacuum locked onto the pile of books and took off in that direction, putting Berbie the Loving Bug to shame with its speed and maneuverability.

With an alarmed squeal, I threw myself onto the

machine just before its sucky parts glommed onto the books and inhaled them whole into its insatiable bag.

I'd already lost two teacups, one bank deposit bag, my favorite pair of sneakers, a bagel with cream cheese and strawberry jelly, a hairbrush, and we'd almost lost Sebille's giant bag to the machine. We *would* have lost it too if all three of us hadn't jumped in to hold onto the bag and wrestle the rabid vacuum to the ground. Sebille had yanked the frayed plug from the wall at that point, and we'd all taken a deep breath in relief. She'd shoved her bag into a cabinet and closed the door on it, just as the vacuum's cable lifted off the ground and inserted its plug back into the wall.

It had been a downhill battle for sanity ever since.

Rolling violently beneath me, the vacuum shoved itself off the floor, nearly managing to unseat me in the process, and fought my tightly-wrapped arms to get to the books.

"Time?!" I shrieked, sweat pouring down my temples and my last nerve unraveling before my very eyes.

"Ten, nine, eight..."

I gritted my teeth and held on.

"Seven, six, five..."

Sebille skidded past, a dancing mop in her arms,

and her red hair sticking up as if she'd snacked on a lighted bulb for dinner.

"Four, three, two..."

The world dipped and spun. The magic-drenched engine beneath me roared, and Sebille's head hit the wall with a hearty, whack, whack, whack as the mop gave it everything it had and then some.

"One!" Rustin screamed.

Nothing changed for a moment. I was still being beaten to a pulp by the determined vacuum. Sebille's head was still denting my wall. And Rustin continued to look out the front window through the eyes of the golden mask, which was clinging to his wispy countenance as if it had been magically glued there by Elmer the glue god himself.

The dividing door slammed open and Wicked shot through on a yowl, Casanova's chair hot on his heels. The chair stopped in the middle of Croakies, turned this way and that assessing its targets, and then propelled itself right at Sebille, slamming into her just as the sun rose over the horizon and every-thing went quiet and still.

I dropped to my butt on the carpet, sneezing as the vacuum coughed out its last, dusty breath. Sebille collapsed under the chair's attack on the back of her knees and sighed, momentarily glad for the chance to rest.

It didn't last long. She soon started shrieking and

jumped to her feet as the chair no doubt molested her and then took off across the store, dancing from leg to leg in obvious pleasure of its coup.

A final, alarming clang announced the theater mask's landing on the table beneath the window.

I scrubbed the back of my hand over my brow, mopping up sweat, and let the breath heave through my lungs. "I'm just going to come right out and say it. I hate Samhain."

Sebille shoved the mop to the floor and leaned against the wall. "Amen and amen."

I looked at Rustin. Around midnight, when the mystical veil that was holding magic back from the natural world had first dropped, he'd had a few minutes to enjoy being almost fully formed. I'd enjoyed seeing the look of wonder on his face as he examined his hands and looked down at his feet, which were actually touching the carpet. Unfortunately, his pleasure had been blasted away ten seconds later by a herd of ghost bison running from two spectral American Indian warriors on painted ponies.

If I squinted, I thought I could still see the hoof-prints compressing his wispy form.

I shoved to my feet with a groan. "I'm going to bed. I'll see you guys in a few hours."

Sebille nodded. "Don't expect to see me before three this afternoon. I'm going to need serious peanut butter and fudge ripple ice cream therapy to get over being made a sex object by that ferking chair again."

I felt my eyes go wide. "You have ice cream?"

She pasted a glare on her pale, freckled face. "Don't even think about trying to beg some. It's going to take every last spoonful of my stash to recover from last night."

I didn't have it in me to fight. I headed toward the dividing door, yawning widely. "Will you check the locks and wards?"

Sebille grunted her agreement, and I started up the stairs to my apartment. A moment later, soft footfalls behind me announced Wicked's arrival. He shot past and slipped through the apartment door, which I'd mostly given up on closing since my cat always opened it again anyway.

The sound of wings fluttering above my head reminded me I hadn't returned the artifacts to their assigned spots. With a weary groan, I turned and flung out a hand, sending my seeking energy toward SB. "Take the sword with you," I told him, my jaw cracking under another yawn.

"Fair seas to ya, Lass."

I saluted him.

A beat later, the mop and the vacuum cleaner floated through the door on a wave of green energy. Sebille trudged through after them, heading toward the spots on the shelves from which the magic had pried them loose. It occurred to me that I could follow her and see where she'd moved her stuff.

I still didn't know where she was living. Only that it was somewhere inside the artifact library. And that it was well-hidden because I hadn't been able to find it.

I hesitated, torn by warring desires to drop into bed versus finally discovering where Sebille was resting her stubborn red head.

Eventually, weariness won out and I trudged upstairs, praying the following night would be better than the last. A prayer that wouldn't be answered.

The coming midnight would be Halloween eve, and the magic veil would be even thinner than what we'd just survived.

Nothing good was gonna come from that.

2

PORTRAIT IN PIMPLE

My sleep was restless, filled with darkness, chaos, and terrifying images. Underlying it all was a dense throbbing in my brain, like the pulse of an ominous heartbeat. I woke on a short scream, my eyes shooting open as the last of the ugliness washed through me.

As soon as my eyes opened, I realized the pain I'd experienced in my dream was real. The bright sun beyond the window sent spikes of agony through my head before I could snap my eyes closed against the assault.

I groaned, tugging the covers over my head in an attempt to hide from the migraine stabbing pickle forks into my brain.

I lay there for a few minutes, my mind trying to form a coherent thought. The attempt was futile. The pain was slicing my reasoning processes into confetti, turning everything but the awareness of its existence into white noise.

The mattress dipped beneath my shoulder, and a low rumble worked its way into my thoughts. Something dented my pillow. Warmth and ease slipped through my skull as a soft bulk pressed against me.

A moment later, I fell back to sleep.

When I woke up an hour later, I found Wicked lying on my pillow, his sleek gray form curled around my head like a hat.

I yawned, stretching, and realized the headache was all but gone.

Wicked had expunged it with his touch.

Miracle of miracles.

It took me another moment to realize what should have been obvious from the start, if only the migraine hadn't overshadowed everything but its miserable touch.

I'd gotten an artifact order!

Something that hadn't happened for a while.

Maybe the Universe had reclaimed its mastery over the artifact process.

I started to sit up and stopped as one of the images from my nightmares flared up in front of my eyes again. But when I blinked, the image disappeared.

That was new.

I waited another minute. When nothing further

happened, I swung my legs over the edge and slipped from bed.

I'd ask Sebille about the nightmares, the headache which Wicked was apparently able to help me beat, and the flashback that felt all too much like an artifact come to life.

Maybe she could help me make sense of it all.

"It was a mirror," I told my assistant and Rustin later. "A pink one."

Rustin frowned. "Did you recognize it?"

"No. Well, I'm not sure. It flashed by so quickly I didn't really get a clear picture of what it looked like."

Sebille slid a book into its proper spot on the shelf. "It's interesting that you received an order today after all this time of no orders. But I don't think we can discount the nightmare and the flashback. Those are new developments that have to be tied to the order."

I couldn't argue with that. Mostly because I agreed. "So when the Universe repaired the order system, maybe it made some improvements?"

Sebille shrugged. "Or maybe the process has been wrong since you took over the library. Maybe this is the way it should have been all along."

Sebille hadn't started working at Croakies until

after I'd become Keeper of the Artifacts, so she couldn't speak to how the process was supposed to run. She and I had come up with a way to succeed under the old parameters, which had been unclear, vague, and more than a little frustrating.

"This might be a reflection on Wicked," Rustin said.

Sebille and I both fixed our attention on the ghost witch. "What do you mean?" I asked.

"I mean that, clearly, Wicked affects your keeper magic. He's able to not only enhance and strengthen it, but he has definite magic of his own. The old process might have been created around a different Keeper, with different tools and strengths. You and Wicked are a unique team. The magical Universe might have adjusted its process to fit the fact that you acquired the cat."

It made some sense. "But then why did it suddenly change again?"

"I have no idea," Rustin said, shrugging.

I sighed. "I guess we'll just muddle through and see what happens. That seems to be my fate."

"It could be the season."

I glanced at Sebille. She slid the last book into place and brushed her hands down her bright orange dress. I grimaced as I took in her bright green and white striped socks, which made her look like a long, thin pumpkin on a striped vine.

She saw me looking at her and frowned. "Maybe

this order was a fluke because the magic veil is thin right now."

"I didn't get nightmares and flashbacks last Samhain," I told her.

She shrugged, walking away as if she'd lost interest in the subject.

Sighing, I pulled the Book of Pages from my pocket, resting it on my palm until it expanded to its full size. I laid my hand over the worn, leather cover and felt the covering warm and roll beneath my touch.

The book flashed open and pages started to flip past. Empty page after seemingly empty page flickered by until it stopped suddenly, two-thirds of the way through the thick tome. A single black splotch oozed up to the surface of the page and then another, and another until lines formed and a recognizable shape materialized there.

I wasn't familiar with the business the book was showing me. The structure was a rectangle of glass and brick, with wide windows displaying the contents of the store to passersby.

The sky above the building was dark, a nearly full moon hanging just above the widespread branches of a large tree to the right of the structure.

The picture shimmied on the page for a beat and then a final rectangle appeared, its surface covered with large letters in bold, squared-off text.

It was a sign. Bearing the words, *Mirror World*.

I left Sebille minding the store and brought Rustin with me. Mr. Slimy insisted he needed to come too, so I put him in his little plastic basket and carried him into Mirror World. I stopped inside the door, realizing for the first time since determining I might be looking for a mirror how big a task it was going to be to find it.

There had to be five thousand mirrors in that place.

I stood staring at the contents of the warehouse, a hundred Naidas glaring back at me from all manner of glass and frame in every possible shape. The sight was as disconcerting as it was disheartening.

Who needs to see a big red pimple growing on her nose in a hundred different mirrors at once? I reached up to touch the vivid ruby mountain near the tip of my nose. When had that shown up?

Banshee blisters! As if the purple arcs under my eyes from lack of sleep weren't bad enough. And what in the names of all the goddess's cats was wrong with my hair? When had that little hump formed on the side of my head?

Clearly, the previous night had done me bad.

"Welcome to Mirror World," a cheerful voice said. "Can I help you find something?"

Yeah, I thought uncharitably. *You can help me find*

a way to shroud all these mirrors before I discover a new flaw to worry about. I turned to the salesman...sales kid, really...and gave him a tight smile. "Hey."

He twitched, blinking hard when he looked at me. "Oh! Wow. I'm really sorry. Car accident?"

My smile turned to a glower in the beat of a heart. "I just want to look around."

The kid shrugged, scratching a nail over his long, pointed nose. "Suit yourself. We're having a Halloween sale."

He jabbed a skinny digit toward the back corner of the warehouse store, beneath a banner depicting a trio of ghosts and declaring it a "Boo-tiful Sale". "Everything under that banner is fifty percent off."

Thanking him, I headed for the sale aisles. It seemed like a good place to start. I determinedly avoided looking into any of the mirrors as I passed, happy only to see my indistinct shape and movement as I hurried past. But as I passed one ornate golden standing mirror, a flash of unaccustomed color caught my eye and I jolted to a halt, my gaze sliding to the mirror.

What I was looking at was definitely scary. But, unfortunately, it was just me.

Rustin materialized next to me, turning the overheated air cool and moist with his ghostly presence. "There's something very dark here," he told me, his tone ominous.

"Of course there is," I said, sighing. "Okay, let's

split up. I'll take this side. You take the other half of the room. We'll meet in the middle."

He disappeared without another word. I clutched Slimy's basket and resumed my trek toward the floor stock arrayed beneath the banner. I stopped in front of the collection of mirrors resting on the shelves, noting that they were all oddly shaped, most likely meant to represent holiday-specific things and creatures.

The pumpkin-shaped mirror was in an orange frame with a thick green stem sticking up from the top. There was a witch-shaped mirror with a pointy hat painted on the glass. When I stared into it, I appeared to be wearing the hat.

Cute.

Not.

Especially since the giant pimple on my schnoz could definitely be misconstrued as a witch's wart.

Next to the witch was a mirror with a frog-shaped green frame. I kind of liked that one, particularly the googly eyes glued onto the frog's face. I opened the lid on Mr. Slimy's basket and let him see. "Look, it's a you mirror."

He eyed the corpulent frame and harrumphed. *If I'm that fat I'm going to have to cut back on the calcium-dusted crickets.*

I chuckled. "You might as well cast your bulgy blacks around these mirrors with me."

I'd recently learned that the frog had kind of a

second sight when it came to magic and supernormals. He'd been able to see through a magically-induced fog to the powerful evil goddess hiding within it.

I walked along the metal shelving unit, holding the frog up so he could view them all. "See anything?"

Not here, no. But that critter up there looks a little hostile.

"Up where?" I swung my gaze along the mirrors on the highest shelves, mere feet below the ceiling. As my gaze swung toward one of them, an ornate oval version with black and gold framing, the surface seemed to shift. But by the time I'd focused my attention on the mirror itself, the glass was empty.

A woman strolled past behind me, and I realized I'd probably just seen her movement in the glass.

Fifteen minutes later, Slimy and I met up with Rustin. "Anything?" I asked him.

He shook his head. "Whatever was here before is gone."

We started back toward the front of the store. The sales kid spotted me trying to make it out of the store and started toward me. I picked up my speed in the hopes I could beat him to the door.

Unexpected, a vision popped in front of my eyes and I stumbled, barely catching myself on the nearest shelf before I fell. It was the mirror again, with one additional detail I hadn't caught before. There'd been a face in the glass, a shadowed one, with hostile blue eyes.

"Is that a frog?"

I looked up into the clerk's pale green gaze. "Um, yeah. It is."

I thought the kid was going to tell me no frogs were allowed in the building. Instead, he got a gooey expression on his face and reached out to chuck Mr. Slimy under the chin. "He's kind of cute."

That critter touched me! Slimy said, horrified.

I quickly shoved him into his basket, closing the lid before the kid decided it might be fun to hold him.

"Can I hold him?"

I shook my head, trying to step past the nosy sales kid so I could get to the exit. "I wouldn't advise it. He tends to pee on you when he gets nervous."

The kid's cheeks puffed as he grinned. "Sweet!"

I narrowed my gaze on him. "Um. Yeah. Well, I've gotta..." I pointed toward the door.

"What do you feed him?"

I bit back a frustrated sigh. "Bugs. He likes bugs."

"My cousin had a boa constrictor once. He fed it rats and stuff. It was cool." He frowned. "Hey, don't snakes eat frogs too?"

The basket started to vibrate. A trembly voice in my head squeaked, *Snakes?!*

I shoved past the clerk. "Snakes eat people too," I told him, raising my eyebrows.

The kid didn't seem to know how to process that little piece of info. His frown deepened. "Not cool, dude."

I took off for the door, relieved to be getting out of the store, and jolted to a stop as I rounded a shelf and came face-to-face with a large standing mirror. The rectangular glass was surrounded by a plain-looking frame of light wood.

A pale face stared back at me. A ghostly face, with wide blue eyes, bumpy brown hair, and a wart-like protuberance on her nose.

As I stared in shock at the spectral-like figure, the wide mouth in the mirror started to curve upward, showing a familiar set of teeth in a snarly smile.

There was only one problem, and it was a big one.

The figure in the mirror was me. But the real me wasn't smiling.

3

HIDING A BODY AND OTHER PERTINENT THINGS

"You saw your doppelganger?" Lea asked, her blonde brows spiking upward. I noted the pale aspect of her pretty round face and the way her hand clutched the counter, knuckles white.

I stood in Lea's shop, *Herbal Remedies with Mystical Properties*. I'd sought her out after returning from Mirror World because I was spooked. I wanted to run the experience past my best friend to see what she thought. "That bad?"

I could see she was trying not to overreact, but it was clear she was having only mild success. "Doppelgangers have..." She grimaced before catching herself and forcing her expression to neutral. "Are you sure the person in the mirror looked like you?"

"Just like me. Same unruly brown hair, same

terrified blue eyes..." *Same ginormous pimple.* I thought about it for a moment. "Well, her eyes weren't terrified, but mine were. And she was wearing my clothes. How does that even happen?"

Lea took that as the rhetorical question it was. She sighed. "I'm not going to lie to you, Naida. This is bad."

The icy spot I'd been nurturing in my heart since seeing the image staring back at me from the glass at Mirror World blossomed, consuming my entire middle. "Bad, how exactly?"

Other than the obvious badness of having a doppelganger show up in my life.

"Many believe doppelgangers portend death or bad luck."

"Do you believe that?" I asked, my voice strangled.

She winced, and that was all the response I needed. I collapsed over the counter, placing my head in my hands. "Crocodile crudités..."

I felt the warmth of her hand against my back. "We'll figure this out, Naida. There has to be a way to settle it without...you know."

I grasped at the bent, soggy paper straw she offered me. "Okay. Can we do a spell or something?"

She nodded. "I'll start researching it. What happened after you saw the spirit in the mirror?"

I blinked. "Um. Well. It just...walked out."

"Walked out? Like *out* of the mirror?" Her voice

had kind of a screechy quality that brought her cat familiar's head up from where she lay in a beam of sun on the floor. Hex eyed her witch through narrowed dark gold eyes for a moment. Then, apparently deciding there was no emergency, flopped onto her back and gave herself over to the sun.

"Not out," I said, shaking my head. "More like out of sight behind the frame."

"So, as far as you know, she stayed within the mirror's frame of influence?"

"Yeah."

"Good. That's good. I'll start there." She nodded, looking thoughtful. Then she lifted her gaze and grabbed my arm. "Your friend in New York, can you talk to her about this?"

My friend worked at one of the big publishing houses in New York. She sometimes got me new releases early as thanks for my having helped her escape a rogue mirror artifact once. The experience had left her permanently changed, turning her into a doppelganger spirit, but she'd managed to keep all her better human qualities intact. Fortunately, her boss, who was a banshee, had been very understanding of her new wispiness. It had been a strange case, but a fascinating one, and it had been a lesson for me on the precociousness of magic. It had also bought me a lifetime friend who knew something about the ins and outs of doppelganger magic.

"I'll talk to Pansy about it. See if she can give me any insights."

Lea squeezed my hand. "In the meantime, stay away from all mirrors. Have Sebille shroud them for you. Just in case."

I left a few minutes later with a heavy heart. With everything that was going on...the thinning magic veil and continued threats from the Société of Dire Magic to strip me of my Keeper of the Artifacts title, I was stretched thin both physically and mentally. I didn't need the worry of a doppelganger spirit on top of everything else.

The scene I walked into a moment later at Croakies didn't exactly improve my mood.

There was a small, well-dressed man standing in front of the door, and I whacked him in the back as I shoved it open. The bell jangled happily above my head as the man grunted in pain. "Oh my goddess! I'm so sorry. Did I hurt...:"

The man turned around, and my apology fell silent.

The face staring back at me made my blood run cold.

Rogers from the Société of Dire Magic fixed a pale blue gaze on me, his lips twisting with disgust. The man's face was narrow and pasty, with a pointy chin that was made sharper by the dark blond goatee marking it.

As he had the last time I'd seen him, Rogers wore

an old-fashioned black suit with rounded lapels and a bowler hat. His thin mustache twitched beneath his nose as he looked at me, making him look like a mouse sizing up a predator. "Miss Griffith."

The simple greeting held more disgust than a year of Sebille's eye rolls, which was really saying something. "Rogers."

"I see things are out of control as usual."

Frowning, My gaze followed his as it slipped toward the sales counter, screeching to a halt on an unfortunate sight.

The hobgoblin sat on the edge of the counter, the golden mask that had attacked Rustin the night before fixed over his face. Hobs' familiar shock of light-brown hair stuck up from behind the mask, and his oversized ears twitched happily as he lifted a small hand with spidery fingers in a wave. "Hello, Miss."

Hobs swung his oversized feet against the back of the cabinets, creating a thump, thump, thump that seemed perfectly designed to annoy the crabby SDM representative.

Rogers flinched with each small, concussive sound.

"Hobs, what are you doing in the store?" I threw Rogers an apologetic glance and reached back to lock the door so no human customers could come inside before I got the hobgoblin tucked safely away in the artifact library. "You know you're not supposed to be in here during the day." The statement was meant for Rogers' consumption. Kind of a CYA move that would actually do nothing to C my A, since the Société seemed determined to shut me down.

I held out my arms and the little creature leaped into them, giving me a hug with his skinny but surprisingly strong arms before sliding to the ground and cocking one jaunty hip. "Miss Sebille is playing hide and seek with me." A high-pitched giggle emerged from behind the mask. "She'll never find me here."

"Here? As in standing in plain sight in the bookstore?"

"No, Miss. Behind this mask. I'm totally hidden."

I frowned. "I don't think..."

The dividing door slammed open and a breathless Sebille ran through, her gaze sliding around the space. "Have you seen...?" She spotted Rogers and jolted into silence. "Um, my favorite pen. I've been looking all over for it."

I barely restrained the eye-roll dancing on my lids. "It's too late, Sebille. Rogers has already seen Hobs."

She frowned. "He has? Where is he?"

I opened my mouth, my gaze sliding toward the small, masked invader. "You mean, you don't actually see him?"

She skimmed a look in the same direction, her

eyes narrowed. "No. Because. He's. Not. Here." She peaked bright red brows, fixing a glare on the SDM rep. "Is there something we can help you with, snitch?"

Rogers' face turned mulish. "Yes, you can show me the library. I'm here to do a surprise inspection." Rogers pasted on a mean smile. "Surprise!"

"On Halloween Eve? Are you crazy? You know everything goes topsy-turvy during Samhain," I squealed.

"I don't know any such thing. Are you telling me you've lost control?"

Sebille growled. I fought the impulse to tell her to stop. If anybody deserved to be growled at, it was the mean and petty SDM rep. "Grasshopper droppings," I muttered.

His mean smile tightened. "Don't swear at me, Miss Griffith. I have the full power of the Société of Dire Magic behind me. One word from me and you'll be stripped of your title. Right now, that word is dancing on my lips. All signs point to the fact that you're a terrible keeper. Reports of fleeing artifacts abound in this dimension. You've lost more humans to poisonous artifacts than any of your peers. And you seem to have a genuinely clueless aura about what you're supposed to be doing, how, and when."

"That's not my fault..." I began, before biting my tongue against the defense I'd been about to mount. Defending myself against the charge of incompetence wouldn't just harm *me*. It would also take down the keeper before me, who'd done a poor job of passing on the keys...metaphorically speaking...of keepership to me. "The Universe has been in flux since I became keeper. There's a fault somewhere in the system."

His pale brows lifted for a beat before he schooled the obvious surprise in his expression. Did he actually think I hadn't noticed the problem? He must truly think I was a gnish. "And now I discover you have a hobgoblin living in the artifact library," he went on as if I hadn't spoken. "Have you lost your tiny little mind?"

Another growl emerged from the Sebille region of the room. "Hobs is helping us. He's not dangerous," she said.

The little guy sidled over to Sebille, pressing against her leg like a frightened toddler. I almost smiled as my hard-as-troll-nails assistant dropped a soothing hand to his tiny shoulder. "He's not going anywhere."

Rogers straightened to his full height, which put him about eye-level with Sebille and at my nose level. But he didn't seem to notice he was too small to frighten anybody in the room except for the hobgoblin. "The rules are clear. Hobgoblins are not allowed in artifact libraries. That...creature must go."

"But..." I attempted to plead my case.

"Or, you can just hand me your keys right now."

My mouth slammed closed. I wasn't handing Rogers the keys to Croakies, and I certainly wasn't throwing Hobs out on his sizeable ears. But I needed time to come up with a solution, so I simply frowned and held my tongue.

"Now, if you'll be so good as to show me into the stacks..." the SDM representative said smugly.

More growling drifted from the Sebille locale.

Seeing no way out of it, I nodded. Sebille glared at me as I passed by, but I lifted my finger in a "give me a minute" signal and she kept her peace until I'd closed the dividing door behind Rogers.

As soon as the door was closed, Sebille rounded on me. "You can't seriously be considering throwing Hobs out!"

"Of course not," I said in a low voice. "But, I need a minute to figure out what to do about this."

"I know what to do about it. There's a swamp in the Enchanted Forest where a body will disappear within hours."

I sighed. And, yes, it might have taken me a beat longer than it should have to reject her solution. But, hey, give me credit for eventually getting there. "We're not offing Rogers, Sebille."

"Better him than Hobs," she muttered crankily.

I didn't remind her that it had only been a couple of weeks since she'd been on Rogers' side of the issue we were discussing. Since that first angry rejection of the hobgoblin, Sebille had realized how much fun it was to have a creature in the store she could fling against the wall like sticky string and have him gather himself back up, laugh, and charge back for more.

He was Sebille's perfect playmate and she was smitten. Hobs was like the opposite-child to her antipodal-motherness. The child of her cranky nature rather than her heart. And Hobs loved to play happy victim to Sebille's creative torture-play.

They were perfect for each other.

"I'm not going to put him out on the street," I promised them both, earning a wobbly smile from Hobs, which I could barely see through the mouth slot of the mask. "I need to look at the rules and figure out how to get around them."

A consummate rule-breaker herself, Sebille clearly liked that idea. "Good. But keep that disappearing body option on the back burner. Just in case."

The front door handle juddered, and I turned to see Detective Wise Grym's handsome face framed in the window. He lifted his brows and gave his watch an exaggerated look. I hurried over and opened the door to him. "Did you close early?" Grym asked, giving me a grin.

I shook my head. "Sorry. Hobs showed up in the store and I had to make sure nobody saw him."

"Too late for that," Sebille said snarkily.

I threw a glower in her direction before addressing Grym. "The Société of Dire Magic decided to show up today of all days for a surprise inspection."

Grym narrowed his delicious dark-caramel gaze. "During Samhain? The Société knows this is magical goat rodeo time, right?"

"Oh, they know," I said, frowning despite my determination to rise above the mean-natured reality that was Rogers. "For some reason, this guy has it out for me."

Grym glanced at Hobs. "It was really poor timing for your little friend there to break the rules."

I chewed my lip, nodding. "He never breaks the rules. I don't know what came over him."

Sebille pulled her shoulders to square and sent a venomous glare Grym's way.

The cop noticed. "I'm no threat to him, Sebille. I'm just stating facts. You're aware of veil poisoning, right?"

I thought I saw a glint of surprise lighting her iridescent green gaze before she hardened against him again. "Hobs isn't poisoned."

"It's common enough," Grym persisted. "Nothing to be ashamed about. He's used to being under somebody's thumb all the time. He might not have known to guard against it."

She shook her head stubbornly, but I saw the speculative glance she gave him.

"What can we do about it, if he's been poisoned?" I asked.

Grym shook his head. "Nothing except manage it. As soon as the veil thickens again, he'll be fine. But there's no cure. Next Halloween he'll suffer the effects again."

4

KILLING CASANOVA'S CHAIR

"Skid-marked mouse panties," I ground out. "How do we know for sure if he's poisoned?"

"Does he have a rash on his face?" Grym asked.

I eyed the mask. "Hobs, can you take the mask off, please?"

He shifted from foot to foot. "Hobs can't do that, Miss."

The first thread of real concern slipped through me. "Hobs, it's important. If you want me to protect you from that mean man, I need to know if you're sick."

Hobs slipped behind Sebille, his long arms winding tightly around her thighs. "I can't, Miss."

I threw Sebille a look. She nodded tightly. Reaching toward the hobgoblin, she tried to make a grab for the golden mask but Hobs skittered away, faster than the eye could follow, an evil cackle drifting in his wake.

Grym's brows lifted and I sighed. "I guess that answers that."

"I'll keep trying to get it away from him," I said.

"You probably won't be able to. He must know the rash is a dead giveaway."

"He isn't dangerous, is he?" I asked Grym, worrying about Wicked and Mr. Slimy.

"The poison exacerbates all his normal characteristics. So if he was mean before, he could be dangerous now. If he was timid, he'll be afraid of everything."

"And if he was fun-loving and mischievous?" I asked, afraid to hear Grym's response.

"He'll be worse on both counts." He must have seen the despair in my face and took pity on me. "It will all be over in a couple of days. Maybe you can lock him up somewhere safe until then?"

I nodded, changing the subject. "What brings you to Croakies?"

"I'm doing some legwork on a vandalism case at Mirror World." He was watching me closely and probably didn't miss the look of surprise on my face. "Every mirror in the place was shattered."

My knees started to give out underneath me and I stumbled toward the nearest chair, dropping into it.

"I'll make tea," Sebille said, hurrying away. Sebille's solution to almost everything was a good cup of tea. But since I was convinced she added a little magic to every cup, she was probably right.

Grym sat down in another chair at the small table where I'd landed. "Part of my investigation was to watch the security tape for the hours leading up to the vandalism. You were on the video." He grinned. "You and your frog."

I nodded numbly. "We were there looking for an artifact."

"Did you find it?"

"No. Well, I'm not sure. But I found something else. Something worse."

"What was it?" Grym's handsome face darkened with concern.

A cup of steaming tea appeared in front of me and I took it, taking a bracing sip before answering Grym's question. "I found myself. No...that's not strictly true. I found my bad side. And I'm pretty sure it's my fault it broke all those mirrors."

"A doppelganger spirit?" Grym asked, leaning forward.

Nodding numbly, I lifted a terrified gaze to him. "What if the shattered mirrors were a message?" I asked him.

"What kind of message? That you made her mad?"

I shook my head, warming my icy hands on the steaming tea. "No. That she's going to find me. And when she does, it's not going to go well for me."

He clasped my hand in his big, square one and gave it a squeeze. "Then we'll just have to find her first."

I nodded, though I had no idea how to go about that. Especially with everything else I was dealing with at the moment. Then I had a terrible thought. "You don't think the spirit did something to Hobs?"

Sebille dropped into the third chair, shaking her head. "Doppelgangers don't inhabit other creatures willy-nilly. That's not their thing. Once the spirit sets its sights on you, it will only represent as you as long as you're around. Nobody else. They're extremely single-minded creatures. Don't forget, this spirit may look just like you, but she's not really you, Naida. She's a demon."

I thought of my friend, Pansy. She wasn't evil. I realized there was probably a lot more to it than Sebille was telling me. "So, I have to die to be released from the thing?"

Sebille nodded. "Generally, yes."

"There has to be a way around that," Grym said, his hand warm around mine.

Sebille frowned thoughtfully. "We might be able to use the thinning of the veil against it. The thinness makes it easier for magic to enter our plane, but in theory, it would also make it easier to force the spirit back into its own plane."

I scrubbed my hand over my face, feeling weary

and not a little bit scared. My life was already a mess. The new threat felt overwhelming.

The dividing door opened, and Rogers shot through with a yelp. He tried to slam the door closed, but there was something in the way. I stood up, afraid it was the spirit.

Unfortunately, it was something worse.

Rogers leaped forward as Casanova's chair danced into the room and scooped him up from behind, rearing onto its back two legs and spinning jauntily as Rogers tried to climb the back to keep from being goosed by the randy furniture.

I hurried forward, intending to help and having no idea how to do that given the fact the chair never listened to me or anybody else. I jolted to a halt as the door swung open again and SB flew through, a bawdy bar song on his beak and a sword sailing through the room beneath him.

I threw out my hand to grab the hilt before it could reach the SDM representative and SB fluttered into the air, shedding a colorful swath of feathers across the bookstore as he flew an exuberant circle through the space.

"May all the blood of all the Brits be spill'd along the shore, for Blackbeard wields a spritely sword as sharp as the tongue of a whore."

"Hush, SB!" I yelled as I fought with the dancing sword. The blade had clearly been infused with an errant strand of magic because it wasn't listening to me at all. I clasped it in both hands, sweat pouring down my temples as I struggled to bring it to heel.

In the meantime, Sebille shot an arrow of magic energy the color of her green eyes into Casanova's dancing chair. The oversexed chair shot into the air, spinning in circles so fast poor, pasty-faced Rogers was a blur, and then dropped hard enough to the ground to eject the SDM rep from the seat and send him crashing into a shelf of books.

The chair went very still, its upholstery drooping.

Sebille and I fixed it with a wary gaze. "Did you kill it?" I asked my assistant.

She shrugged as if it didn't matter one way or the other to her. "Hopefully."

A long, drawn-out groan reminded me I hadn't dealt with my real problem yet.

Rogers shoved slowly to his feet, his bowler hat sideways on his head and his tidy jacket askew on his shoulders. He lasered me with a deadly gaze, scowling so hard he was in danger of his goatee popping off his face. "You!" He lifted a short, shaky finger in my direction. The quivering digit was permeated with such rage that if it had been able to fire a bullet, the ammunition would have pierced my heart and kept going until it had seared through several walls before finally being subdued.

"I'm really sorry..." I said before being cut off.

"You *will* be sorry," he gasped out, tugging his

hat around with a quick, slashing movement. "You will be very sorry indeed, Miss Griffith." With that he stomped toward the door, grasping the handle and twisting it hard enough to separate it from the wood.

Rogers' hat popped up from his head and then dropped, popping up again a moment later. A muffled "ribbit" emerged from under the bowler. Rogers went very still. "What is under my hat," he ground out slowly.

Sebille snickered.

A flash of movement atop the bookshelves had me turning my head in time to see Hobs cocking a finger and blowing on the tip.

I wanted to cry. Instead, I trudged over and removed Rogers' hat, handing it to him so I could grasp the fat green squish on his head with both hands and pull him safely off.

I peed on his head, Slimy said with a blink of his blank, black eyes.

Sebille snorted out a laugh, and I gave her wide eyes. She covered her face, coughing into her hand as Rogers turned to share his hatred with her. "You two would be smart to begin searching for new employment and a different place to live. Your time here at Croakies has a very short shelf life...pun intended." He jammed his hat back onto his head and left, slamming the door behind him so hard the glass rattled.

I read somewhere that frog pee is good for the scalp, Slimy added helpfully.

A determined cracking sound filled the silence. I watched as the window in the door sported a diagonal fissure that ran from the top left corner to the bottom right corner.

I dropped into a chair at the little round table, the frog squatting on my thighs. Depression made my limbs heavy and I fought tears.

The frog hopped closer, settling into a soft puddle in my lap. He didn't say anything. I got the feeling he was just there to give me comfort. I appreciated the thought, if not the actual fact that the leaky amphibian was perched on my leg.

The other chair was suddenly pulled out and flipped around. Grym sat down on it backward, his dark-caramel gaze finding mine. "It's going to be all right, Naida," he told me in a soft, rumbly voice.

I shook my head, not realizing until a tear slipped off my chin that I'd been crying. "It's going to be over soon one way or the other. Either the doppelganger will kill me, or the SDM will throw me out into the streets and I'll die of starvation since I have no marketable skills."

Grym patted my hand, sighing.

A steaming cup of tea appeared before me, I looked up into Sebille's glower. "Stop being such a drama queen," She said. "We're going to kick this thing's phantom, doorstopper-sized behind, and then we'll tackle the SDM."

I took the tea, sipped it, and sighed. Somehow I *did* feel better. Despite the reference to my doorstopper-sized backside the doppelganger was reflecting. I smacked my lips. "What's in this? My tummy feels all warm and stuff."

Sebille winked at me.

Seeing her wink, Grym held up a hand. "Yes, please."

Sebille was chuckling darkly when she headed back to the tea center.

I eyed Grym. "What do you know that I don't?"

His smile was wide. "I saw what she put into the tea."

I opened my mouth to ask and then decided against it, taking another sip of the delightful concoction. Ignorance was bliss at the moment, and goddess knew I needed a little bliss.

I staggered up to my apartment a short while later, the room spinning slightly but my mood greatly improved. Grym had promised to repair the glass in the front door, and Sebille was going to confer with her mother about my doppelganger problem.

I felt a little better. Until I realized it was only a

couple of hours until the witching hour returned and my battle with all the artifacts in the library would begin.

Then there was Hobs...

No. I wasn't going there. I'd think of a way to contain him until the veil thickened later.

Right after my nap.

Stumbling into my apartment, I headed straight for my bed, dropping onto it face first and letting the whirling inside my head spin me to sleep. Sometime before I dropped completely off, the mattress dipped and a warm, soft presence curled into my side.

The gentle rumble of Wicked's purring lulled me the rest of the way into oblivion.

5

PUMP ME UP

*S*leep wasn't restful. I jolted awake an hour later and sat bolt upright, my head aching. I groaned, rubbing my temples, and climbed out of bed with two thoughts in mind. I needed something for my cottonmouth, and I needed to talk to Grym.

Oh, and I needed to sing the Make Me a Magic Muffin song too. As soon as I realized that, I veered toward my bathroom, the third thing taking precedence over the others.

Fortunately, I'd covered all my mirrors as soon as I'd learned about my unwelcome friend. Still, I ducked under it on the way into the tiny bathroom and washed my hands in the kitchen instead of standing at the bathroom sink.

After the dreams I'd had, I wasn't taking any chances.

I sucked down two glasses of water and then

headed down to the store, hoping Grym was still there.

I found him shaking the glass man's hand and hurried over as the man picked up his toolbox and headed outside. "How much do I owe you?" I asked Grym as he closed the door.

"Nothing."

"I don't want you to pay..."

Grym held up a hand, stopping me. "He wouldn't let me give him anything. I helped him out once, and this was his way of thanking me."

I walked over and eyed the man as he slid the wooden box full of tools into the back of his truck. He spotted me and gave me a wave.

I waved back. "Is he supernormal?"

"He is." Grym stood beside me, grinning. "But I'm not going to tell you what he is."

I narrowed my gaze. "As long as he's not a giant stink bug, I'm okay." I'd recently had a too-close encounter with a giant stink bug shifter and I hoped never to experience that particular level of disgusting again.

Grym's smile widened.

So did my eyes. "No!"

Grym just chuckled darkly. "Sebille brought back tacos. We left yours over there on the table."

I fell on the treat with a groan, realizing as I smelled them just how starved I was. "Oh, these taste so good." I looked around. "Where is she?"

"In the greenhouse. She and Queen Sindra are researching a solution for the doppelganger problem."

I nodded, running the napkin over my lips. "I have an idea about that. And I need your help. Can you get me into Mirror World?"

He frowned. "Are you sure? It doesn't seem like a good idea for you to be around a bunch of mirrors right now."

I nodded, gathering my wrappers and stuffing them inside the paper bag. "You said they were all smashed, right?"

"It sure looked like it to me."

"Then it should be safe. Mostly. I think there might be one mirror in there somewhere that wasn't broken. It could be my artifact."

He frowned. "Then it's not safe. I'll go and see if I can find it."

"No!" The word came out much harsher than I'd planned. I closed my eyes and took a deep breath. "I'm about to lose my job because I suck at it so bad. I need to do this. Wrangling artifacts is *my* job, not yours. I'll take precautions. But I have to go with you."

When his frown softened a bit, I tried gentling my tone. "Please, Grym. This is important to me."

He held my gaze for a moment and then sighed. "Okay, but how are you going to keep from meeting up with that thing in the mirror?"

I swung my gaze toward the open dividing door, and then around the room. Placing my finger against my lips, I quietly walked over and closed the door, sending my keeper magic into the knob to keep anyone from opening it except me or Sebille.

It was possible my cat, who seemed to have more magic than I did, could open it from the other side. But I was counting on the fact that I'd left him curled up on my bed, out like a light.

I did the same with the exterior door. Then I walked over and opened the cabinet under the tea things, pulling out a small, white paper bag with a big grease spot on it.

I opened the bag and almost passed out from the delicious aroma wafting up from inside.

Grym peered inside the bag, lifting a dark eyebrow in silent question.

I shook my head, pulling the frosted chocolate brownie out of the bag and placing it on a paper plate.

I leaned close to Grym and spoke softly. "Be ready to grab him."

He didn't bother to hide his confusion, but he stayed close to me as I walked over and set the plate down on the table.

I barely had time to wave my hand over the plate a few times to spread the delicious aroma through the air before the illumination overhead segmented, and I was bathed in a light breeze as something flashed past.

I looked down in dismay.

The brownie was gone.

Fortunately, when I looked at Grym, he had a rocklike arm wrapped around the little hobgoblin, who was trying to shove the brownie through the narrow, inflexible mouth hole of the mask.

I reached out and tugged the mask off Hobs' face. "I'll take that, thank you."

Hobs shoved the brownie into his mouth, his cheeks bulging accordingly.

He grinned, chocolate covering his small, sharp teeth.

I grinned back. "Good?"

He nodded.

I took his little hand, spidery fingers warm against mine. "Hobs, you've been poisoned by magic." I pointed to the telltale rash over his cheeks and he frowned. "You're sick."

The hobgoblin swallowed and twined his long fingers tightly around my hand. "Yes, Miss. I don't feel so good."

"I know, Hobs. You're not going to be able to keep your promise to me and be good over the next couple of days. So we need to put you someplace safe. Do you understand?"

He looked worried but nodded after only a slight hesitation. "Hobs doesn't want to be bad, Miss."

"I know. Will you let me keep you and Croakies safe?"

"Yes, Miss."

"Good. Wait right there." I dialed Sebille's number and waited until she answered.

"What? I'm busy."

"Too busy to save your little buddy?" I turned the phone so she could see Hobs. He had chocolate spread all over his lips and chin, and his teeth were still brown with it when he grinned at her and waved.

"I'll be right there."

Twenty minutes later, Hobs was safely locked away in a shrink-enchanted metal box, which had once held a miniaturized dragon and currently held a miniaturized hobgoblin and a pile of brownies. Sebille had also given Hobs her phone, so he could play games, surf the net, and call her when he ran out of brownies.

I was feeling pretty good about my solution for one problem, at least.

Now on to the next one.

Grym was using the key he'd gotten from the owner to open Mirror World's front door. "You look ridiculous in that thing." He pushed the door open and indicated I should enter in front of him.

I adjusted the gold mask, *feeling* ridiculous. "I know. But it will keep me safe, no matter what we find in there."

He nodded as I stepped through the door. "I have to admit it is ingenious."

"Why thank you, kind sir." I gave him a shallow little bow. As I moved into the store, my shoes crunched over seemingly endless shards of shattered glass.

I stopped and looked out over the huge space, horrified by the extent of the damage. "Woodpecker knees," I murmured. "This is horrible."

"That's a lot of rage," Grym offered.

I couldn't disagree. "The thinning veil must have amped the thing up."

We stood looking around for a moment before Grym spoke up again. "Where do you want to start?"

I tried to remember the dream that had inspired me to return to Mirror World. It was hazy and vague, not helpful at all. "I'm not sure. Let's start in the back room. Maybe they keep some mirrors back there for repair or something. They might have been missed."

"Good thought." He pointed toward a distant gray metal door. "Manager's office is back there."

I followed him back, both of our heads on a swivel. "Did you speak to the manager when you were here before?"

"No. Just the kid who was working here."

I was glad the kid was okay. He was annoying,

but he didn't deserve to die at the hands of a nasty doppelganger spirit.

I didn't see a single mirror in the enormous place that hadn't been shattered. The devastation was complete. Even the bigger, heavier mirrors on the high shelves around the walls were shattered, a few of them had even been knocked over in the assault.

I settled a sad glance on the frog-shaped mirror and frowned. Maybe I'd ask the manager if he'd sell it to me anyway. I could always get new glass for it.

The thought made me smile.

Grym pushed through the door into the stocking and office area, and we looked around. Glass sparkled from the long, plywood-topped table in the center and caught the overhead fluorescent light from the floor. It wasn't nearly as bad as the devastation on the floor of the store, but all visible mirrors had been broken the same way. There just hadn't been as many of them.

"I bet that's more mirrors." Grym pointed to several large boxes leaning against the wall across the room. "I'll start there."

"Okay." I jerked my chin toward a door on the sidewall. "I'll go check the office while you do that." I left him to muscle the boxes off the new stock and headed for the open door and the golden light that spilled out onto the bare concrete floor beyond the doorway.

I was shocked to see the mess inside the office.

Papers were strewn about the floor. The room's only chair was toppled and torn, as if someone had stomped on the seat with cleated shoes. Or ripped it with claws.

I shuddered. I hadn't thought a doppelganger could climb out of a mirror unless its target was on the other side. Could the thinning veil have given the thing extra zing?

I saw no mirrors in the office, but a cheap print of a bunch of dogs playing cards was on the floor, the glass inside its frame shattered. That glass had probably broken when the print hit the floor, rather than at the hand of an angry doppelganger.

Still, I gave the glass and the print a wide berth, skirting the desk with the intention of checking the desk drawers.

I didn't quite make it to the drawers.

I jolted to a stop as I rounded the desk, finding a woman's shoe on the floor near the overturned chair. It was a pretty pump. Sage green with a two-inch heel. And it had a woman's foot inside of it.

6

ANNOYING WATER WEIGHT

"Grym!" I screamed, backing away so I didn't spoil the scene. "I need you in here, stat!"

Heavy footsteps hurried my way, and the detective suddenly filled most of the doorway. "What's wrong?" Even as he asked the question, his knowing gaze slipped over the room, cataloging all the signs that violence had invaded.

I backed toward him, pointing toward the barely visible heel near the desk leg. "I'm guessing that's the manager."

He reached toward the small of his back and pulled out a gun. It surprised me. I hadn't realized he'd been carrying one and wondered why he pulled it after the fact. Then I realized. If the manager had been recently killed, the killer could still be in the store.

The thought made me step away from the door, putting the wall at my back.

Grym crouched down beside the body and felt for a pulse. He gave her a quick, cursory examination and then stood, his gaze dark with concern. "No signs of what killed her. But I smell sulfur." He slipped the gun back into the holster he must have fitted in the small of his back. Either he didn't believe she'd been murdered or...

"This was a magical death." He lifted his right hand, which had been hidden from view beneath the desk. He was grasping a pink, circular object in a folded sheet of paper so his prints didn't mar the surface. He held it up and I saw the lid canted out at a little less than a ninety-degree angle.

I realized with a start what it was. "A compact." A sour-sweet smell wafted past my nose. A scent like almonds and burnt sugar.

He nodded. "With a mirror."

His statement hung between us, like acid on the air. The small office suddenly felt stuffy and claustrophobic. Fear seared through my belly like a burning lump of coal. "It's loose," I said, speaking so softly I was surprised when he nodded.

"It would appear that it is," he agreed, frowning.

"Great globular goblin slobbers."

Light sheered off the mirror beneath the paper wrapping, slanting across the space between Grym and me and then dissipating into nothing.

"Yeah." He nodded, lifting the compact. "The good news is that the spirit has taken this poor woman's form. You should be safe."

I took a long, shuddering breath. "I wish that was true," I told him, lifting a hand and sending out a wisp of keeper magic. The chime came quickly since the "artifact" was mere inches away.

The compact jerked itself from Grym's grip and floated over to me. It hung in the air between us, waiting for me to snatch it up. "I'm afraid we're all still very much in danger." I reached out, my fingers poised around the compact but not making contact.

"Don't touch it," Grym growled. "It's evidence."

A distant chime tinkled against my hearing, and I made a mental note to check it out later.

The compact disappeared in a puff of black, sulfurous smoke. My fingers closed on nothing. Only a tingle against my skin told me it had been there at all.

His eyes went wide. "What just happened?"

I sighed. "It wasn't the true artifact. Just a representation of one."

He canted his head. "You've seen this before?"

"I've read about it. I'm afraid this is a product of the thinning veil. The doppelganger magic is skewed. It's not working the way it should."

A soft puff of sound had Grym and me turning toward the body just in time to watch the woman's clothing flutter to the floor, empty.

"Instead of taking on a physical form, the spirit is removing the physical form of its victims and turning them into doppelganger spirits."

My knees wobbled. I leaned more heavily against the wall. "And the more the magic goes bad, the more the spirit will try to gain the form it seeks."

"Meaning?" he asked, his broad shoulders drooping.

"Meaning, this thing has the potential to take out a lot of innocent victims. If I don't figure out how to stop it."

An explosion ripped through the silence. I ducked instinctively as dust and debris rained down on my head.

The ceiling opened up and a white, plastic pipe dropped out of it, pouring liquid down to drench the floor beneath our feet.

I grabbed a binder from the desk and held it over my head, shielding myself from the worst of the water.

Grym grabbed my arm and we hurried out of the office. Unfortunately, the growing puddle of water followed us out, lapping at my heels as I ran toward the door into the main store. It raced past me, hitting the space in front of the door and rising up until a pale, familiar face wavered on the glassy surface made of water.

Grym's gun hand came up, but the figure inside the makeshift mirror smiled. It wasn't a nice smile.

The detective's gun would be useless against a spirit.

"Hello, Keeper," a voice that sounded almost like mine said. The tone was much harder-edged than I believed mine was.

I shoved the mask closer to my face, hoping the elastic band holding it there held. "What do you want?"

My doppelganger spirit laughed cruelly. "Why, I want you, Naida keeper. I want your blood running through my veins. I want your power strumming through my cells."

I almost laughed. She was going to be sadly disappointed if it was power she was coveting. Unless she had a thing for making people pee their pants. Looking into her mean-natured face, I figured she probably did.

"That's not going to happen, spirit," Grym said. "So let's come up with a Plan B, shall we?"

She cocked her head, the smile sliding away as a cold light filled her blue eyes. I noted the thin band of gold encircling them and wondered if the spirit's true form was bleeding through the image. The eyes widened, darkening to navy and skimming speculatively over the detective next to me. She licked her lips. "I think I'm going to like this body. Does *he* come with the package?"

"Yes."

"No!"

Grym and I answered at the same time. Unfortunately, we didn't answer the same way, pretty much negating both our responses.

We shared a quick look, and he shrugged before turning back to the spirit. "Your power will weaken soon, spirit. The veil thickens again after midnight tomorrow. Do you want to work with us to look for a solution? Or risk being locked forever into a form that can't be fully realized?"

The girl who looked like me on a crabby day crossed arms over her chest. "I'll bite, Detective Grym, why can't it be realized?"

"Naida's a KoA. Do you really believe the Powers That Be would allow you to possess a Keeper of the Artifacts?"

Normally, he wasn't wrong. I didn't have much in the way of magic energy, but as keeper, I did have some magical protections from the Universe.

The figure in the water mirror laughed gaily. "The PTB have no clue what's going on. And even if they did, they're surely aware the SDM is set to oust her as Keeper." My doppelganger shook her head. "No, this creature is mine. It's only a matter of time before I claim her."

My mouth fell open. How could the spirit have known? A prickling sensation skittered over my skin, settling in the base of my spine like a block of ice. I would have argued the point, but my gobsmacked expression probably would have made it impossible to convince anyone.

Goddess bless him, though, Grym tried. "You've been listening to the rumor mills. That's a mistake, spirit. Rumor isn't truth."

The doppelganger's arms dropped to her sides. "Maybe not. But it represents the edges of truth." The water in front of her lifted and she walked forward, her shape wavering in the crystalline form of the water she rode.

The golden rings around the eyes thickened for a beat and the face elongated, turning beak-like before it returned to looking like my evil twin. A deep and uncomfortable worry niggled in my churning belly. A new concern, though undefined, to squabble with the already overwhelming apprehension of being inhabited by a doppelganger spirit.

The water rushed my feet, the spirit mere inches from me before I could blink. Instinctively, I knew that if she touched me, even the mask wouldn't be enough to save me.

I jumped to the side, ducking away as a burst of water shot in my direction, a disembodied hand enveloped beneath its glossy surface. The liquid dropped to the floor, spreading quickly in search of my feet.

Barely escaping the spirit's touch, I bolted for the door. I jumped over the stream of liquid, turning as I made it through the door to make sure Grym was on my heels.

I didn't see him.

Where had he gone?

Panic welled inside me, tightening my chest until it felt as if my heart was dying beneath my ribs. I retreated back into the work area, my gaze searching for Grym.

The water dropped to the floor and rose again as the spirit adjusted to my movement. The doppelganger's murderous gaze locked on me as it rose again. "You're just wasting time, Keeper. Let's get this over with. I have so much I want to do, and I'm tired of cooling my heels waiting to do it."

I shook my head, glancing surreptitiously around for a sign of Grym.

Had the spirit done something to him? I wish I knew what they were capable of. In my ignorance, I was helpless against it. I took a step toward the oval-shaped water mirror, holding the spirit's gaze but letting my peripheral vision search for the detective.

I finally saw him. Movement beyond the watery reflection. Grym's form was wavery and shifting behind the water, but it was definitely him.

He held something long and slender, curved on one end, in his hand. His other hand was outstretched, a pink circular object sitting on top of his big palm.

The pink compact? How could that be?

Grym's gaze lifted and found mine. He held what I recognized as a crowbar above his head and snapped the compact closed with his thumb, lifting it and nodding.

I caught his meaning, moving closer. The spirit watched me come, speculation thick in her gaze. "I'm not going to set you free," I said, to distract her from what was happening behind her. I only hoped cold iron worked on doppelganger spirits like it worked on ghostly spirits. Hopefully Grym knew more about it than I did.

Which wasn't really saying much.

"It's not really up to you, is it, Keeper?"

The voice changed, turning more petulant, almost whiny.

I danced sideways as the water on the floor shifted and then jumped, using my piddly keeper magics to give me a boost as I leaped onto the large, wooden table.

"Now!" I screamed as the spirit adjusted direction, the water plunging to the concrete and then surging upward to face me again.

Grym threw the compact in my direction. I lifted my hands as the doppelganger started to turn, the water beginning to drop to the floor, and prayed to the goddess I wouldn't fumble-finger the thing into the concrete and break it.

The spirit flashed back, facing Grym, as the compact hit the tips of my fingers and bobbled into the air, its trajectory adjusted toward the water-riding doppelganger.

"No!" I threw out my keeper magic, a silvery ribbon spitting from my fingers, and the compact jerked to a stop mere inches from the floor. I tugged it toward me as Grym swung the iron bar toward the spirit, a channel of deadly moisture sheering toward me with an unexpected burst of speed.

With a panicked cry, I bent backward at the waist, the glistening droplets of death barely missing me. I wrapped my fingers around the compact just as the droplets hit the plywood tabletop and sizzled there, jerking in my direction like a marionette on a string.

The crowbar hit the glossy tower of water and severed it horizontally through the middle, water spraying everywhere as the spirit's form folded inward and then exploded out into the room in a million glistening droplets that fell over both Grym and me.

I tensed as it hit me, but fumbled with the clasp of the compact until it opened, and spread the two halves wide as I held it in front of me.

The column of water spun like a typhoon on the ocean's surface, the energy it created flinging paper and dust and small boxes filled with Styrofoam peanuts everywhere. I braced as the shape inside the water began to pull free, the edges of the spirit inside seeping from the water as the cyclonic energy built to an impossible intensity.

"Hold on to it!" Grym shouted. "It's going to hit with a lot of force."

The spirit shot free of its watery cocoon and crashed into the mirror, hitting me with the force of a bullet that slammed the small, pink compact closed and sent me flying backward off the table.

I screamed as I fell, expecting pain when I landed. Instead, I touched down with a loud crunch and a spray of foam peanuts into the air. I just lay there, my knuckles white on the closed compact and peanuts filtering down to ping off my face.

I was butt down in a large box filled with packing materials, my legs dangling over one side and my arms jammed up around my ears with the compact clutched in one hand. I shifted in an attempt to unjam myself, but I was stuck fast.

Heavy footsteps approached.

I blew a foam peanut from my lips as Grym's handsome face peered down at me. He grinned. "Going somewhere?"

"Yeah," I said, swinging my arms. "Slap a few stamps on this box, Detective and send me someplace warm and boring. I need a vacation."

A moment later, I was standing next to the box, pulling peanuts out of my bra and the waistline of my jeans. I held the artifact up to him. "Where'd you get this?"

"I heard the second chime earlier and figured it was somewhere in this room. I saw it when I went to grab the crowbar."

I nodded, examining the well-used compact. "The woman and the other compact were decoys. They were never real."

He nodded. "That thing. That's not a doppelganger spirit, is it?"

I frowned. "Technically, no. Although, I'm guessing that, whoever is using it to try to get out of the mirrors is really a spirit of some kind, looking for a body to inhabit."

"That's an actual artifact?" He asked, nodding toward the makeup mirror.

"It is. A very dangerous one. It will be going into the toxic magic vault at Croakies."

He nodded. Glancing at his watch, he said, "I need to go check up on the manager, make sure she's okay. Do you want to come with? Or should I just give you a ride home?"

"I'd better go home. It's going to be dark soon, and the magic's going to go crazy tonight. I'm going to have my hands full keeping it all contained."

We headed into the store and toward the exit. Beyond the glass, the sun was low and the coming night was hazy. It would be full dark sooner than usual.

Buzzard blisters. Just what I needed.

We shoved the door open and I stood staring up

at the dying sun as Grym locked up behind me. A distant throb, throb, throb sent a jolt of quick fear through my system. The sound of wings on the air. I often heard that sound in my nightmares and imagined I heard it throughout the day. With the magic so fractured and unexpected under the thinning veil, my imagination was working overtime.

"Ready?" Grym asked, a warm hand on my back.

I nodded. It wasn't until we climbed into his car that I remembered him saying *Yes* to the spirit's question about being a package deal. I turned to him, my gaze narrowed in thought, as he pulled out of the lot.

What had he meant by that? Was he implying he thought of us as a couple? "Surely not," I murmured aloud before I realized it. "Oops. Sorry, Shirley," I said as the air started to roil in front of me. The tiny pixie hovered over me, her eyebrows a judgmental slash beneath the tight pin-curls of her dirty blonde hair. "Sorry, I didn't mean to call you."

She pounded the air with her drab brown wings and glared down at me. "Make up your dang mind, you derf!" And then she disappeared again, leaving behind a cranky command not to call her.

Grym slid a glance my way. "What's her deal?"

I shrugged. "She doesn't like to be called." However, as the supernormal world's version of Witch-a-pedia, with fun trivia and occasionally useful information about all the magical families and their ancestors, I was pretty sure Shirley got called a lot.

Grym pulled his boxy car up to the curb in front of Croakies a few minutes later. I slid out, bending to look through the door and thank him before I went inside.

I stopped at the entrance to Croakies, gripping the handle with trepidation and taking a deep, bracing breath. I was becoming terrified to enter my own store. Things always seemed to be cray-cray lately.

With another bracing breath, I turned the knob and stepped inside.

7

PREDATOR UNDER GLASS

a hand snaked out and grabbed my wrist, yanking me inside.

I yelped in surprise and stumbled as my assistant all but threw me across the room. "What the...?"

"Shhhh!" Sebille peeked beneath the shade she'd pulled down over the freshly repaired window in the door. "Come here," she whispered.

Rubbing my sore wrist, I headed over and stood beside my crazy assistant. "What's going on?"

She slammed a hand over my mouth. "I told you to shhhh!" She pointed to the window, her eyes gleaming iridescent green in the near dark.

"Why are all the shades closed," I asked.

She huffed out an impatient breath. "Can't you just do as I say for once?"

I shook my head, but leaned forward and pulled

the shade aside, peering out into the growing darkness.

At first, I didn't see what she was talking about. The thick form of the massive predator was just another notch in the distant roofline, like an owl-shaped gargoyle hulking high above the street in search of unsuspecting prey.

Then I realized what I was looking at and jerked backward. "The enforcer!"

Apparently, *we* were the prey. Sebille and I. And probably everyone we cared about. "She's back."

Sebille paced the floor behind me, her eyes eerie green orbs on the air.

My eyes went wide. "Lea!"

"Already taken care of. She and Hex are in the greenhouse. They've created a giant cloaking ward that's like an owl-sized bug zapper. Margot won't attempt to get to them. Especially when her real target is here."

Croakies. Me. One of us a huge source of magical gold and the other, a chance for sweet, sweet revenge.

"We need to get to the greenhouse," Sebille told me almost angrily. I could tell by the look on her freckled face that she expected me to argue.

"I'm not leaving. I can't desert my post."

She huffed out a breath but nodded. "I thought you'd say that."

The air grew hazy and cool. Rustin's tall form

rose up between us. His lips were compressed into a straight line, and his eyes were dark with concern. "As far as I can tell, she's alone."

I swallowed hard. "Then, it's definitely her?" I asked as my last hope dissolved.

"How many other giant owls do you know?" Sebille snapped crankily.

I forgave her the crabbiness. She was tense and probably a little scared. I'd be cranky too if I could push past my initial emotion of terrified. "Okay. We need a plan."

"Here's the plan," Sebille said, glowering at me. "Run."

"Okay," I said, giving her a quelling look. "We need a Plan B."

She sighed. "I was afraid you were going to say that too, so I have an alternate plan."

The dividing door slammed open and I jumped, screaming, my hand flattened protectively over my heart. Mr. Wicked's soundless prowl through the door was definitely anti-climactic.

"That's your plan?" I asked, crabby finally fighting its way to the surface.

"What? That?" She snorted. "No, Naida. Don't be stupid. He's just an annoying cat."

"Yowl!" Wicked said, not liking her attitude at all.

I didn't blame him. "Then what is your plan?"

"We set the anti-Quilleran locks on the front door and the dividing door and then hunker down in the library. Whatever happens out here, we don't open the door."

"She'll completely destroy the bookstore," Rustin said.

Sebille shrugged. "Acceptable losses. We can't save it all."

I hated her idea. And I knew I'd need to come up with a better one. But danged if my over-stressed brain could develop one.

Before I could think of a solution, something hit the front of the store, and the glass in the big window rattled until I was shocked it didn't break. I looked at Sebille.

"Reinforcing magic," she told me.

Nodding, I glanced over at Slimy's tank. "Where's the frog?"

"He's with Hobs," Sebille told me, her gaze sliding away from mine. I would have asked her what she wasn't telling me, but another concussive force hit the front of the store. We stumbled sideways as the very foundation rumbled.

The first crackling sound was insignificant, but it quickly grew until a spider-web of cracks covered the entire surface of the glass.

"Sebille!" I screamed as the giant predator slammed into the glass again, clearly having determined it was the weakest point of entry.

"It'll hold," Sebille said, her hands coming up and green light flaring outward in a wash that smoothed and repaired the cracks before my eyes. "For now."

I felt my eyes go wide. "For now?"

"Obviously, we need to stop her from just banging into it until the wall crumbles," Sebille snarled.

"Right. Yeah. Plan B. I'm working on it."

"Work faster," Rustin said as the wall shook under another blast. Dust filtered down on our heads and I sneezed.

Wicked jumped up onto the counter and sat on the leather-bound book there, his eyes an orange glow in the dusty dark. He wasn't purring, which was always a very bad sign.

But I recognized his thought process. We just needed to figure out how to get Margot there.

"Okay, here's Plan B. We let her in."

"Have you lost your beady little mind?" Sebille and Rustin asked in unison.

I held up my hands. "Hear me out. We let her into the store, where she has limited maneuverability. We distract and keep her busy long enough to trap her." I moved behind the counter and pulled the giant bottle of bubbles out from the shelf beneath Wicked. "With this."

Sebille's gaze narrowed. "The magic trap you used on Hobs?" She shook her head. "That's not big enough to hold her, Naida."

"Not the one I used on Hobs. This is one I

ordered to replace the one Theo gave me. I got the extra big one. Don't ask me why. I just did. It should hold her long enough to use this." I poked my finger onto the surface of the ancient leather book Wicked was draped over.

"The Book of Pages?" Sebille frowned and then her expression cleared. "You want to send her into the abyss?"

"Yes."

"But you destroyed the clocktower page," Rustin said.

We'd sent his evil Uncle Jacob into the abyss beneath a giant clock tower that continually measured the last moments until Midnight. Once we had the wicked witch in there, I'd torn out the page and destroyed it so he couldn't escape.

"There have to be other pages for the abyss," I said, frowning. It was a weak point, I knew. I hadn't had time to explore the option with everything else that had been going on. "Can you try to find one?" I asked him.

He nodded, moving quickly across the room on wispy feet that didn't touch the ground. He reached out a hand and the book lifted off the counter. Mr. Wicked jumped to the ground with an irritated meow, and the three of them disappeared into the artifact library.

"So how are we going to keep her busy?" Sebille asked.

A wisp of sound was all the warning I got as an enchanted wine glass, filled with a rich burgundy wine flew through the connecting door and headed right for me. I flung up my hand and caught it, red liquid sloshing onto my hand. I took a sip. "We unleash the Kraken," I told her with a tight smile. "We might as well go with what we have."

In the distance, a rusty roar announced the reanimation of the insatiable vacuum cleaner.

Sebille sighed. "Let the games begin."

I was going to use a keeper magic that I hadn't wanted to attempt in the past. I still wasn't sure if I could manage it without doing all sorts of unintended damage. But I was the mistress of Croakies and, as such, my powers inside the store and the library were superior.

"Are you sure?" Sebille asked me for the third time. "You've never done it before."

And it could be catastrophic. Yeah, I got that. Which was why my belly was filled with biting eels at the moment.

Not literally, of course.

Though who knew. That might be the end result of me using the unknown magic. "Alice assured me it could be done." I frowned, trying to remember the previous Keeper of the Artifacts' instructions when she'd been sort of training me. "I have it in my notes somewhere."

"We don't have time for you to go off and study," Sebille said on a sigh. "It's a miracle the place is still standing."

She wasn't wrong. Over the last half hour, the giant owl outside had bashed almost continually against the brick building housing Croakies until I was pretty sure I was going to discover that it was cracked all over, like a hard-boiled egg before you peeled it.

It was a good thing the few human businesses on the street had closed up a couple hours earlier, the employees no doubt heading home to prepare for Halloween costume parties.

"Use your instincts," Sebille said as another blow hit the building, higher that time, near my apartment. "They've served you well to this point."

Fresh sweat bathed my palms. I nodded, closing my eyes, and tugged on the strands of keeper magic infusing the store. The potential for magic in the place was immense for someone who was tied into its flow.

And as Keeper of the Artifacts, I was.

Theoretically.

In my mind, thick strands of silvery magic floated toward me from the walls, the floor, the ceiling. The magic undulated on the air, like ribbons floating down from a great height, and eased softly through my pores, gathering at the core of where my magic waited to be expelled.

It was a pleasant sensation, not overly invasive, but also not enough. I would have to tap into the vast stores waiting for me in the artifact library to do what I planned.

The idea terrified me. I wasn't afraid I wouldn't get enough magic to do what I needed to do. But, I had no built-in regulators to help me control the flow. The energy would likely slam into me like a freight train, rather than easing into me in a manageable flow.

A particularly onerous concussive force slammed into the building and I was thrown forward, onto my knees. The large window shattered, glass flying through the room in a wash of green fairy magic.

I couldn't do anything about the window in that moment because I'd tugged tentatively on a thread in the next room, and a tsunami of energy was flowing in my direction.

On some level, I was aware of the throb of wings, the wash of cool October air forming a brittle cocoon around me, and the warmth of Sebille's magic as it swelled to deal with the broken glass.

I had to trust her to seal the window.

And I had to trust myself to complete my magical task.

I shoved to my feet, pressing forward with my

teeth gritted and my hands outstretched, shoving the tidal wave of energy toward the massive bookshelves filling the center of the space.

I was vaguely aware of movement around me. Of the occasional jarring pain as something connected with my exposed limbs. But I had to keep my focus locked on shoving the power I'd gathered against my enormous target.

Somewhere deep inside my brain was the kernel of certainty that, if I didn't expel that energy into my goal, it would burn me up from the inside.

Slowly, steadily, the enormous shelves shoved across the space, compressing and coalescing as the magical energy bathed them in a spongy web of magic preservative. Slowly. Steadily. Until the outermost shelving unit thumped into the furthest unit and began to ooze into it, becoming a solid, compacted wall with an impermeable surface.

I hit my knees as the energy glazed over the outside shelving, cocooning the thousands of books in an impenetrable wall of magic.

Still, the energy poured into me.

Sweat poured down my face, and my hands shook under the enormous power. In my minds' eye, ribbon after ribbon of ravenous energy drifted toward me, and I had no way to shut it down. I had no tools to make it stop.

I tried closing off my magic, but it was locked in

the "On" position, accepting everything the artifacts in the library wanted to give me.

I heard a strident voice screaming my name from a distance, but I couldn't cut through the dense fog of magical energy to respond.

I couldn't even stand.

The hard carpet burned my knees as I fought against the magic pulling me toward the compacted shelves. I realized with a stark wave of pure fear that, if I didn't find a way around it, the magic would encase me in the bulwark I'd created too.

"Naida!"

Something hit my shoulder. Hard. An annoying shriek penetrated my eardrum. I jerked my eyes open to find myself inches away from the wall, and Sebille wrapped around me like last year's rejected sale coat.

"Banshee blisters, Naida! Snap out of it before you turn yourself into a wall!"

The building shook and I jolted in surprise, my gaze sliding to the window I'd been pretty sure had been breached.

I licked my lips. "I..." The words got caught in my throat. I swallowed a ball of cotton and tried again. "I can't stop it."

Sebille released me long enough to smack me upside the head. "Did that help?"

I glared at her. "No, why would it...?"

"Because it made *me* feel better," my ever-compassionate assistant said. She smacked me again.

"Hey! Stop hitting me..."

She slapped me a third time, hard enough to snap my head to the side.

"Sebille!" I jerked out of her grasp, the energy finally oozing away from me.

She nodded, shoving to her feet. "You're welcome."

"I'm not going to thank you for smacking me in the head," I told her as I stood, groaning as pain pulsed through my bleeding knees. I stared at my torn, bloodied jeans, wincing. "That's gonna leave scars."

"We don't have time for you to cry about your boo-boos," Sebille said in her usual uncompassionate way. "We've got to deal with this."

"This?" I straightened, turning around to examine the damage. The building seemed intact. Including the window I was pretty sure I'd heard break earlier.

But my pleasure at that realization died a horrible death as I saw what was going on in the bookstore.

8

AN ABUNDANCE OF CHAOS

*I*t appeared that when I'd yanked the magical energy from the artifacts, I'd also yanked the artifacts themselves.

The air and floor were thick with artifacts of all kinds. Every one of them animated and creating their own unique chaos in my bookstore.

"Oh, no."

"Yeah, Naida. Oh no. It's going to take us all night to fix this."

Sebille ducked as a plate slashed past, her hand shooting up to grab the artifact from a 1950s era television show called, Andrew of Mayberry. The plate overflowed with a steaming meal of roasted meat, mashed potatoes smothered in brown gravy, butter-glazed corn, and a thick slab of buttered bread.

When Sebille grabbed for the dish, the food slid

off onto the carpet. The plate immediately righted itself and refilled, the smell of home-cooking a pleasant counterpoint to the sulfuric stench of the magic. "Stop dancing away from me, you gnish!" Sebille yelled at the plate, which did a little jig on the air and then scooted away when she lunged again.

The companion plate, a matching snack size with a fat triangle of pie nestled on its flower-painted surface, joined the fun, dancing around Sebille's grasping fingers as she tried to snag it.

With a whistle and a song, Cinderella's wand flashed into the room, stopping above the mess on the rug and shooting it with magical stars that created bubbles over the mess but didn't do much else.

Something slammed into the back of my legs. Yelping in pain, I looked down to find the insatiable vacuum cleaner, chord aloft, trying to suck my shoes right off my feet.

I managed to get my hands wrapped around the thing's handle and tried clicking it off, but it jiggled with amusement at my efforts. Okay, maybe the soul-sucking artifact was right to laugh in my face. If the thing didn't need electricity, it certainly didn't care if the power switch was on or off.

I sent keeper magic into the rogue vacuum and started it rolling toward the back. We were thwarted at the door when a full suit of armor clanked into view, its bulk filling the entire doorway and blocking our entrance to the library.

The vacuum tried to bully its way past, getting a massive sword in its dust bag for its efforts. I managed to dive out of the way in time not to get skewered, but the suit of armor kicked the vacuum out of the way and moved into the store, dropping into a battle crouch and brandishing its sword at the flying artifacts.

"Stop that!" I screamed, sending keeper magic into the armor in an attempt to keep it from destroying the other artifacts.

The magic did nothing. Which normally wouldn't surprise me, but since I'd just compacted the entire contents of the bookstore, I'd kind of believed I had some extra juice in the tank.

The armor slashed at Cinderella's wand, earning a face full of soapy water for its troubles.

"Help!"

I spun in time to see Dr. Osvald fly by, his head perched atop one of his magical volumes like he was riding Aladdin's carpet.

The armor turned as I did, its metallic hand with the sword lifting to take a swipe at Osvald. I couldn't let that happen. I had no idea what the result would be if the strange doctor's head was severed from his tomes.

My hands found the edges of the open book and yanked it down a second before the broadsword slashed through the exact spot where it had been.

I hit the ground hard, having no hands to catch myself, and rolled as the sword slammed into the spot where I'd landed.

The book snapped closed as I rolled, shutting Osvald safely inside.

I jumped up and hurried toward the door, sending the book on its way back to the shelves in the library on a ribbon of keeper magic.

"Incoming!" Sebille screamed.

I sucked in a breath and spun in time to get smacked in the face by a colorful conglomeration of brightly-hued feathers and bleeped words. I reached up and caught SB before he could float on past, not realizing until I'd stopped his forward motion that I was looking at his feet.

Hanging upside down in my desperate grip, SB let loose a new burst of foul language, thankfully bleeped to protect the innocent. "Bleep me to bleep and drive a bleepin' blade between my bleeping eyes. What in the name of bleep and bleepnation is going on, Lass?"

"Chaos?" I offered as the sound of metal clanking on metal brought my head up. The suit of armor was in a frenetic battle with Blackbeard's sword, deadly blades slashing dangerously through air that was filled with dozens of roiling artifacts.

A woman's plumed hat from the 1800s dodged

away from an errant slice of broadsword, losing the tip of its plume in the process.

Cinderella's wand dove on the feather tip as it floated toward the ground, covering it in soapy magic.

I carefully flipped SB over and glanced around for a spot where he'd be safe. He took the decision out of my hands by lifting his wings and flying to my shoulder.

A red-tipped feather floated into my hair as he landed.

The building rumbled under renewed impact from our problem outside the walls. I fought weariness and frustration. Scrubbing a hand over my eyes, I took a deep breath and closed my eyes, striving for calm.

Something hit me on the back of the head.

Something else barreled into my knee.

I fought to keep my concentration, my mind searching for a solution.

Glass broke, showering inward with an explosion of force that sent bits and pieces of it into my exposed flesh.

Sebille yelped and I turned to find her bleeding from a dozen different spots. "You okay?"

She nodded, "But not for long." She jerked her head toward the enormous creature flying through the broken window.

Margot Quilleran, the enforcer for the deadly

Quilleran witches, had broken through the wards and made it inside Croakies.

There was no way this was going to turn out well.

The suit of armor charged the massive owl, blade outstretched.

The big predator backpedaled its wings, deadly talons flashing out to wrap around the metallic arm, wrenching it sideways and off with a discordant squeal of tearing metal.

The bird dropped the metallic arm, still clutching its sword. The armor pushed mindlessly forward, ramming Margot and shoving her back toward the window while her wings fought to maintain her forward momentum.

The magic vacuum dove on the discarded metal limb, its ravenous mouth sweeping, sweeping, sweeping until the hand and hilt of the sword had disappeared into its rabid sucky parts.

I glanced toward Sebille. She nodded, disappearing in a flash of green light. A beat later, my assistant popped back into view as a tiny winged Sprite, energy roiling the air in a verdant fog around her as she prepped her magic to use against the witch in owl form.

I looked around at the tea-trays, random shoes and boots, metal boxes, books, a bicycle, a typewriter, and even a woman's makeup desk moving around the store on invisible currents of magic, and realized I had a decision to make. I could use the artifacts to confuse and distract the witch so we could subdue her. But if I did, I risked harming or losing some of them.

That went against everything inside of me. It was at odds with my role as Keeper of the Artifacts and against my better judgment. I realized with a sinking feeling that I couldn't do it.

Enormous claws clasped the still pressing suit of armor and wrenched it away from the owl's breast, flinging it across the room.

I had to jump to the side to avoid being swept away with the armor.

Huge wings pulsing slowly on the air, the predator settled to its feet. Margot suddenly loomed over me, her bird-shaped head cocking and her enormous eyes riveted on me with clear hostility.

I backpedaled as she moved closer, her bulky form more graceful in the confined space than it had a right to be.

Behind her, Sebille gathered the cloud of energy she'd built and threw it at the owl. The magic smashed against Margot's broad back, flaring as it touched the mottled, brown and white feathers, and the owl's step faltered.

For just a beat, the image of a deadly predator wavered, showing the dark, angry face of Margot Quilleran. Her gold eyes were pinched with rage. Her lips were taut with it.

But the image faded quickly, returning to the

white-faced owl. Faster than lightning, Margot's deadly, curved beak snatched at my middle. Agony flared outward from the strike, and bright blood gushed from the wound. I fought to stanch the blood with one hand as I tried to climb to my feet and find cover.

Another green ball of energy burst against the owl's head. With a screech of anger, the witch swung a huge wing toward Sebille, sending her flying across the room to smack hard against the wall.

The owl's head spun all the way around to eye its downed prey. Disturbing. I saw the gleam of interest in the owl's eyes and realized I needed to distract it, or Sebille would become the creature's midnight snack.

"Hey!" I yelled, climbing slowly to my feet. "Over here, stupid."

The bird's head swiveled back around to face me.

I tugged a strand of keeper magic to the surface and let the energy fill my eyes, turning them silver. I knew they'd be glowing, and I was counting on that fact to intrigue the witch. Crooking a bloody finger in her direction, I forced a smile of challenge onto my face. "Come and get me."

The owl's head snapped forward, the beak missing me by inches.

I blinked when I realized I was standing by the counter.

Santa's slippers! How had I done that?

Soft warmth spread over my ankle. Mr. Wicked purred against my calf.

When had he arrived?

The owl's head spun again. I crooked my finger, and the thing launched itself from the ground.

The world shifted, and I closed my eyes on a wave of dizziness.

When I opened them again, I was standing near the front window.

The owl was near the sales counter, its head swiveling to find me.

Fascinating.

The air altered beside me and Sebille burst into her human form, a large, red welt swelling on her forehead. "What just happened?" she asked.

I wished I knew.

Movement above the owl caught my eye. A small whirlwind spun atop the upper cabinet where I kept bookmarks and other sales supplies. The cause of the dervish was unclear. It was moving too fast to see. But the action caught the owl's eye and she stepped closer.

Unseen by the distracted predator, a familiar haze rose from the floor. I watched in fascination as Rustin lifted his hands, and the giant bottle of bubbles appeared on the floor just behind the owl.

The dervish stopped spinning and I looked into the sparkling blue eyes of my hobgoblin, joy turning his gaze bright. Faster than the eye could follow, the owl shifted forward, deadly beak snapping over the spot where Hobs was standing.

When she reared back, he was gone.

I screamed just as Rustin clapped his hands and the mixture in the plastic bottle of bubbles rose upward, encasing the owl in a glossy prison that rose all the way to the ceiling.

Magic flared brightly, snapping taut as the owl tried to lift its wings and was constrained by the magical column.

The owl pecked frantically at the magic encasing her, but the bubbles flexed beneath the attacks and snapped immediately back into place.

I ran forward, my desperate gaze scouring the cabinet. "Hobs!" I turned as Sebille joined me. "That witch ate Hobs!"

The witch in question shuddered violently and cast off the owl. She fell to one knee, head lowered as if the action had been too much for her to manage.

I stared at the pale, brown-haired figure crouching inside the magic trap, feeling my eyes bulging out of my skull. "No. It can't be."

Sebille sucked in a gasp, gripping my arm. "Naida, that's..."

I swallowed hard.

The figure's head lifted, familiar blue eyes found mine, and lips I'd grown up with curved into a mean smile. "Hello, Naida."

The voice was almost the same. But there was a bite to it. Apparently, Margot Quilleran hadn't quite been able to cast off her rage and bitterness when she'd taken my form.

"You're the doppelganger spirit," I said, my voice a dazed drone in the room.

The smile widened. "You finally understand."

My head was shaking before I could stop it. "No. I don't get any of it. What's happening?"

Sebille's grip lessoned on my arm. I heard her sigh. "I think I understand."

I turned to her because it was easier than staring into a face that was mine but wasn't really mine.

Sebille's gaze stayed locked on the witch. "Casting off the four-dimensional glamour Lea put on you was devastating, wasn't it Margot? I'm guessing that you almost didn't survive it."

The doppelganger's determined smile tightened.

"Your physical form died in the effort, didn't it?" Sebille went on, heartless. "All you've been able to conjure up for a physical presence is the owl. Which, I'm sure is okay sometimes, but you've gotten used to being a witch, haven't you? You like being human. You enjoy the perks. You miss your daily tea."

The woman in the bubble winced. The tea was a weak spot with Margot. It was what had gotten her caught in the first place. "You're all going to die for what you've done to me."

Sebille snorted. "Says the woman who has no

physical form of her own and who's caught in a magic trap."

If the taunt was in any way discouraging to Margot, she didn't show it. "I won't be here long, Sprite." Her gaze slid to me. "Not if you want to see your little rodent again."

A jolt like a physical pain sheared through my chest. She was talking about Hobs. "He's still alive?"

Her smile was just about as mean as it could be. "Maybe."

I thought I might pass out. But I forced myself to shake my head. "I'm not playing this game with you, Margot. You're too dangerous to let loose. Even as a doppelganger."

Margot laughed.

The sound made me stiffen, horrified. She was much too sure of herself for my comfort.

"Naida!" Sebille's voice ripped me out of my worried musings, and I whipped my head around. I found her and Rustin fighting to keep artifacts from escaping out the broken window and floating down the street.

"Ghoul boogers!" I yelled as the spirit in the bubble prison cackled meanly.

I looked quickly around for a specific artifact, finding it hovering too near the window.

"Grab the wand!" I yelled to Sebille as I reached for the magic that had nearly overwhelmed me before and threw it out like an energy blanket to coat the remaining artifacts. I had no time for finesse, I needed to work fast. So, I wrapped the energy around all visible artifacts and tugged, dragging them with me toward the connecting door.

When I opened the door, Wicked shot through on a yowl. I had no time to figure out why he hadn't opened the door for himself. He was fully capable. I stepped through the door and yanked on the energy contained within my fist, dragging all of the captured artifacts through and flinging them into the library's cavernous space.

I slammed the door, hurrying past the still-smug witch spirit. "Such a terrible keeper," she said, making me clench my jaw against a rebuttal. I didn't have time to fight about stuff that didn't matter in that moment.

I ran toward the outer door. "Close it up!" I yelled to Sebille.

I saw the tell-tale flair of magic as Wicked and I surged through the door. Glancing up and down the street, I spotted several magical objects sailing glee-fully along the buildings, occasionally banging against the brick or glass looking for a way inside.

I tried to tug on my newly found magic, but it didn't come. Probably because I was no longer inside Croakies. Frustration made me clench my fists and swear again. "Ghost giblets!"

I stood there quivering, a giant ball of stress and frustration, and watched the artifacts drift away from me. Something golden cut the darkness a block away. Moonlight flared on the surface of an all too familiar golden mask. It was moving awkwardly in my direction, with starts and stops and jerky changes of direction.

Then I noticed the dark-clad form struggling beneath it.

"Goddess, no!"

The mask had attached itself to a victim.

The hole in the front window snapped into place again, solid and smooth, and the door behind me opened. Sebille shot out onto the sidewalk, panting. Rustin oozed out behind her.

"Do you need help?" my assistant asked.

I gestured toward the retreating magic. "Several things escaped down that way."

She took off running.

Rustin hesitated, his gaze locked onto the career-ending form lurching toward us. "Is that?"

"Yes," I said too quickly, fighting back tears. "It is. Go help Sebille. I need to deal with this alone."

"Are you sure?" the ghost witch asked me.

I nodded. "I'm sure. Please, Rustin."

A moist, icy touch caressed my shoulder, and then he was gone.

I turned and quietly closed the door, locking it and setting the wards. And then Wicked and I started down the street.

A strange calm had pervaded me. I'd enjoyed

being a Keeper of the Artifacts. I'd miss the magic and my friends. I had no idea what would become of any of them. If I was lucky, the SDM would allow me to deal with the current mess before they showed me the door.

Wicked bumped against my calf, purring loudly. I glanced down. "You're very optimistic as we approach the end of the world."

He swatted my leg, claws partially unsheathed so they bit painfully against the bare skin of my ankles. I couldn't work up any concern about it. I was too focused on the problem ahead.

The figure juddering clumsily down the street stopped suddenly as he heard my voice. "Naida keeper?"

I bit back a sigh. "Yeah, it's me. Let me help you..."

He lifted small hands, his head bobbling as if the mask was too heavy to hold up. "Don't touch me!"

"Don't be silly. You need that off your face, and I can take it off."

He jumped as I touched the mask.

"Hold still."

"It won't come off, I've been trying..."

I sent a ribbon of keeper magic into the spot where the center of the mask molded toward his hair, the mask came off with a soft pop and a puff of air.

Rogers from the Société of Dire Magic stared up

at me, blinking. His too-pale face was uncharacteristically red and sweaty. "Oh, thank the goddess. I didn't know how I was going to get out of there. It pinched me and had a strange smell."

I knew the smell he was talking about. It was Eau de Hobs. I'd smelled it when I'd worn it before. "Sorry, I'm afraid we had another leak at Croakies."

His small face pinched. "I warned you, Naida keeper. You'll lose your position for this."

"I understand. You're right. I've botched everything horribly. I don't blame you for being mad." Though, I suspected that the reason he'd had the encounter with the mask in the first place was that he'd been coming to try to catch me in a Samhain-induced mess.

Dirty pool.

Rogers huffed and chuffed, looking unsure how to continue berating me in the face of my total acceptance of abuse. "Well..."

"If I could, I'd like to ask one favor before I leave."

He tugged on his tie and frowned, blinking rapidly. "I don't believe you've earned any favors..."

"I realize that. But I'm begging you, please. All I want to do is finish out this season and set everything right again for the next Keeper. Will you let me stay until the end of the year?"

Rogers glowered, shifted on his tiny feet, and harrumphed a few times, his goatee quivering. He finally nodded. "Unless you have another crisis. If that happens, we'll remove you immediately."

I nodded. "I understand. Thank you, Mr. Rogers."

It's a wonderful day in the slug-slurping neighborhood.

9

OWL IN A BUBBLE

"What are we going to do with that?" Sebille asked, pointing at Margot.

I turned a frown on my assistant. "How did Hobs get out here? I thought we'd agreed he should stay locked safely away."

Sebille's gaze skimmed away from me. "We did. But I didn't want him trapped in that box if the enforcer..." she sent a glower toward the slightly less cocky spirit in the bubble.

I sighed. If I'd been thinking straight, I probably would have come to the same conclusion. If Margot Quilleran had managed to overwhelm us and got control of Croakies, poor Hobs might have been trapped in that box forever. Or worse. I shuddered to think what that nasty witch would do to a creature that had been trained in the fine art of subservience all his life.

"Ribbit!"

I glanced down at Mr. Slimy. It was impossible to miss his not-so-subtle reminder that he'd been in the box too. Turned out the frog didn't even need words to annoy me. I sighed. "Okay, I forgive you. But it leaves us with a terrible problem. Assuming that she didn't lie to us about Hobs..."

"A huge assumption," Rustin said. "In the realm of making an A-S-S, out of you and me."

I shook my head, refusing to believe Hobs was gone. "He's alive."

Rustin and Sebille shared a look I chose to ignore. "We need to put Margot somewhere she can't hurt anybody."

"The Book of Pages?" Rustin asked.

"Jacob's already there," Sebille said, shaking her head. "Unless you found another abyss where we can stash her, we can't put her there."

He shook his head.

"Sebille's right. Putting them together in one spot is very dangerous," I added. "No, we need to figure out if we can stuff her back into the mirror and then block her from coming out again."

"I can talk to mother," Sebille offered. "Nobody knows more about the mirrors than Sprites."

I nodded. "That's a good idea."

Wicked had been bathing his paws on the table as we talked. But he suddenly jumped up and ran toward the dividing door, smacking his paw against it and hissing.

"What's wrong with the cat?" Sebille asked.

"I don't..."

The lights flickered off and came back on, flashing blue as a shrill alarm sounded throughout the shop. Sebille and I covered our ears, surging to our feet.

"Toxic vault breached," a female voice announced loudly enough to rise above the din. "Toxic vault breached."

"No!" I ran toward the door and reached for the handle, wrenching it open as Rogers' words came back to me, slithering through my mind like snakes. *Unless you have another crisis.* It wasn't possible. What else could possibly go wrong?

As soon as I cracked the door, I stopped breathing. The room was filled with artifacts, thousands of them, all roiling around in the air or sliding across the ground. When I stepped into the library they all changed direction and headed for me. I couldn't allow them back into the store. That way lay complete and utter disaster.

Wicked slipped through the crack before I could slam it shut. "Wicked! Come back here." He ignored me as only a cat can do. I pounded my fist against the door and screamed. "Now my cat's in danger," I wailed, horrified at the whiny, defeated sound of my own voice. "I have to get in there!"

"How?" Sebille asked. She was pacing back and forth, wringing her hands, as the siren continued to bellow and the cultured-sounding female voice continued to berate us for our inactivity.

"The Book of Pages," Rustin said. The blue warning light flashing over his wispy form made him look dead.

I shuddered.

"That's your solution for everything," Sebille said.

My eyes flew wide. "No, he's right. I can take myself right into the vault with it." I hurried over to the sales counter, digging around in the jumble of stuff on the shelves beneath the counter for the book. I was pretty sure I'd jammed it in there earlier.

I couldn't find it!

I turned an astonished look on Rustin. "Please tell me it didn't fly out the window with the other artifacts."

He blinked, looking in that instant too much like the frog for my comfort. "Um...it didn't fly out the window with the other artifacts?"

"There was no conviction in that statement, Rustin!" I yelled. "None at all."

"That's not fair, Naida..."

"Toxic vault breached."

Was it my imagination, or was the disembodied female voice becoming shriller?

Sebille shook her head, lips twitching. "No, she's

right, frog witch. There was no conviction. You didn't make me feel it. I want to feeeeeellllll it in my bones." She crossed her arms over her chest and dropped her head back as she said the word feel.

"You suck worse than that irritating magical vacuum cleaner," Rustin ground out.

Sebille snickered.

"If you two are done bickering like toddlers..."

"Toxic vault breached!"

Nope, not my imagination. Definitely shriller.

"Is somebody going to deal with that?" the woman in the bubble whined, sounding enough like me to make me decidedly uncomfortable. "It's giving me a headache." Her lips curved upward. "I get a lot of those."

"Shut it!" I yelled at Margot. "Nobody wants to hear from you."

"Meowrrrr," the witch said, laughing.

Sebille blasted air through her lips, managing to roll her eyes at the same time. "It's in my purse. I figured better safe than sorry since tonight was supposed to be a bit witchy."

"Sebille, I love you!" I ran to grab her enormous canvas bag from the cabinet under the old-fashioned cash register. I grimaced at the sight of all the coins and paper money spread across the floor. There'd been so much chaos I hadn't even noticed when the magic in the register decided to join the fun.

Unfortunately, there was no time to clean it up. I

needed to get to the vault. Placing my hand on the covering of the book, I closed my eyes as the leather warmed and rolled beneath it. "Toxic magic vault," I told the book.

Pages flipped, carrying me a quarter of the way through the book, and then an image of the vault, magical door awry, opened up on the page. The sight of that door made my blood run cold. I didn't stop to think about what I was heading into. I couldn't. Because the mirror from the evil witch was unshrouded in the picture.

And Wicked was standing inside the door, facing off with it.

I slammed my hand down on the page of the book and felt the magic tear into me, twisting and wringing my physical form until I didn't know up from down. Then it sucked me into the book, ripped me through the void enveloping the tome's magic, and dumped me back to reality inside a familiar spot. I landed hard, rolling across the center of the vault and smacking up hard against the legs of the mirror.

"Meow," Wicked said, running over to sniff my face. "Meow?"

I shoved upward, looking around for the missing shroud. "No, I'm not okay, Mr. Wicked. You scared a hundred years off my life. What are you doing in here? And how did this shroud get removed?"

I located the shroud after a quick search and

grabbed it. It had been pushed under the bottom shelf. Shoving to my feet, I held the shroud over the mirror and glanced around, finding all the artifacts in place. My gaze swung to the door, spotting the telltale shimmer of magic Lea had created as a backstop for when we needed to get inside the vault and we were worried something inside might try to get out. Or, as in the last time it had been used, when we were worried a certain hobgoblin might try to get in.

Thinking of Hobs made me frown. Sadness made my stomach churn. We had to find him. He had to be okay.

"Naida?"

My head jerked around in surprise. A pleasant face stared out at me from inside the mirror. Inquisitive blue-gray eyes sparked with pleasure. The woman inside the mirror waggled fingers painted a feminine hot pink at me at grinned. "It's nice to see you again. How are you?"

I felt my eyes go wide. "Pansy? What? How?"

She tossed her head, covered in messy blonde curls, and laughed, the sound resembling wind chimes on a breezy day. "I felt an impulsion and here I am." Her hands lifted into view. She nodded toward Wicked. "I have a feeling that little guy's behind it."

"Wicked?" My voice was filled with censure. It was one thing to play his little magic games with me, but dragging my friend into it was unconscionable. He stared back at me, seemingly unconcerned that he'd irritated me. "I'm so sorry," I told Pansy. "We have kind of a situation here."

Her gaze slid past me, noting the flashing blue light sending fractured shapes over the iridescent wall of magic currently holding the vault intact. "I can see that." She sighed. "It's the thinning veil, isn't it? This time of year wreaks havoc. I've had to chase off three new ghosts and a goblin dressed as a librarian just today alone."

Pansy worked at the publisher's office by day and lived above a historic library by night. She considered herself the "real" librarian in the place and seemed to barely suffer the human librarians who worked there.

"A goblin librarian? That's a new one. Why would a goblin want to hang around books?" I asked.

"Oh, it wasn't a goblin. Just a really unpleasant woman who looked too much like one for there to be a difference. Believe me, I was doing the kids a favor getting rid of her. She snarled at them so badly one tiny tot peed himself in fear."

I frowned. "Aw, that's mean."

"Right?" She shook her head.

"So how'd you get rid of her?" Despite the trauma of my night, I found myself getting drawn into Pansy's story. She had that effect on people.

"I could have created a little cold spot that followed her around all day." She blinked innocently. "I also might have flash-frozen her coffee a couple of times."

I laughed with my friend. "Perfect."

"Yeah," Pansy's smile slid away, and she focused on my face. "Now tell me what's going on and how I can help."

I was happy to oblige, starting at the beginning with the visit from Rogers, and taking it to the current predicament, or predicaments plural. By the time I wound down, Pansy was frowning in thought and the warning light was gone. Along with its annoyingly, repetitive verbal alarm.

She nodded. "First of all, I can't believe you let a hobgoblin move into Croakies." She laughed with delight. "How deliciously non-traditional of you."

"Yeah, let's see if I survive with my job intact before we decide how delicious it is."

"No, I've already decided. When you get the chance, I want to hear all about him."

I nodded.

"But for now, I'm guessing you're looking for a way to expel both the doppelganger spirit and this witch?"

"I am. Any ideas?"

"Well, first, I'll tell you that this witch isn't a traditional doppelganger spirit. Like me, she was created, or created herself it sounds like, by magical means. Like me, she's retained her own personality and, before she was captured, was managing to retain at least one of her physical forms."

I nodded. She was right. I hadn't thought about it that way.

"So, technically, despite the fact that she's been using the mirrors, she's really just a regular spirit. Not a doppelganger. She's most likely able to take an ethereal form like I do, but she's using doppelganger magic to try to gain a permanent physical form."

I stared back at Penny's attractive face, gobs-macked. "Slug snot! You're right. I've been looking at this the wrong way, entirely."

She nodded, looking pleased with herself. She had a right to be.

"I need to do an exorcism spell," I exclaimed, realizing the solution might be much simpler than I'd thought. I didn't need to send Margot to the abyss. I just needed to give her a one-way pass into the ether. "Thanks, Pans. I owe ya one."

"No, you don't. I'll owe you for the rest of my life, girl. Don't ever think differently."

I started to shake my head but she held up a finger, arching one dark-blonde brow. "Stop it now. Or you and I are going to have a problem."

It was her fiercest librarian voice, and it was barely scary. I laughed. "I wish I could give you a hug right now."

She leaned closer until all I could see was the width of her flat chest. When she reared back again, she had a mischievous look on her face. "Consider yourself hugged."

"Thanks. I'll call you when things quiet down so we can chat."

"You do that."

I threw the specially warded black shroud over the mirror and hurried out of the vault.

Wicked was already in the main area, batting at coins and paper money floating around with the artifacts I'd banished there.

I stood in the center of the huge space and looked up. Feeling a fist of despair clenching my heart at the emptiness above me. It looked like a good eighty percent of the artifacts had decided to join the fray.

Alligator armpits. Cleanup was going to take me the entire three months I had left.

10

NO MORE STINKIN' ARTIFACTS

*S*ebille called the fairies in the greenhouse to transport the magic trap holding Margot Quilleran to the toxic magic vault for extra protection.

I had no doubt that, given enough time, the tricky witch would find a way to escape her prison, but I wasn't too worried. I didn't plan on giving her that much time.

Queen Sindra sent word that she'd reached out to her magical contacts for a solution to the Margot incarceration problem, but she hadn't yet found one. It seemed the time of year, with the wacky magic running rampant, was a serious problem.

Didn't I know it?

With a heavy heart, I left Sebille and Rustin to do the best they could to manage the chaos and firmly closed the dividing door to keep errant artifacts from bursting free again.

I leaned against the door for a long moment, perusing the smaller, but still considerable mess in the bookstore.

Just looking at it made me weary. Especially the compacted shelves. I wasn't looking forward to dredging up the energy it would take to pull them apart again.

My eyes slid shut as a headache began to pulse behind one eye. I panicked momentarily, thinking it was an order coming in for a new artifact.

I didn't need any more stinkin' artifacts!

Okay, deep breaths. It was just a headache. Little wonder since we'd had almost nothing to eat or drink all night. We'd been on our toes and on the run through the full eight hours. Even with that, we'd still been unable to do more than just manage the chaos.

Not a very satisfying night.

The sun finally popped over the horizon at 8:11 AM, and all the artifacts dropped where they were, leaving a jumble of magical items covering nearly every spot in the library.

Well, every spot but on the shelves where they were supposed to be.

Sigh...

Sebille stuck her head through the dividing door and announced that she was going to try to get the first unit of shelves re-ordered before she went to bed. I nodded, so weary my mouth couldn't even form words.

A knock sounded on the front door fifteen minutes later. I looked up from the debris I was sweeping together into a tidy pile, panic flaring that I'd forgotten to put out the *Closed* sign. I couldn't let a customer into Croakies in its current state.

There was no way I could explain the compacted shelves to a non-magic human. Fortunately, the sign was up and the face in the glass at the top of the door definitely belonged to a supernormal.

I opened the door, greeting Grym with a tired smile. "Hey."

Something smelled delicious around the detective, and my stomach growled loudly. He grinned, holding up two large bags and a box from Sebille's and my favorite donut shop. I snatched the box. "Oh, my goddess! You're my absolute favorite person!"

He stepped through the door. "Where's Sebille?"

I couldn't answer because I'd already jammed a donut into my mouth, so I pointed toward the dividing door.

Grym left me to chew and opened the door, calling out that he'd brought breakfast.

I'd known Sebille could move. But with an empty belly and a long night of hard work as her only fuel, even I was surprised by how fast she made it to the store. She skidded through the door, sliding past Grym on a growl of pure need and grabbing the bag he held away from his body as if in fear of losing a limb.

She stuffed a crisp, golden potato cake into her mouth and moaned, even as her fingers dove back into the bag for a breakfast sandwich.

We didn't talk for a full fifteen minutes.

Grym started picking up debris and setting some of the heavier stuff back into place. He stopped in front of the magical vacuum cleaner, eyeing it skeptically. "How old is this thing?"

Sebille and I shared a look and were just tired enough to burst into hysterical laughter. However, to Grym's detriment, neither one of us wanted to stop eating long enough to respond.

He reached for the handle of the vacuum and jumped as the thing grabbed hold of a final spark of residual magic and plowed forward, trying to pull his big boots into its sucky parts.

Grym gave it a karate chop in the dust bag and the thing wound down into silence, its bag deflating.

Sebille and I burst out laughing again.

He glared at us. "I think you two need tea."

"Yes!" we both screamed, spewing crumbs onto the carpet in our enthusiasm.

It wouldn't be as good as Sebille's, but I didn't care. I'd even drink my own burnt and stale tasting tea at that point. I just didn't want to stop eating to do it.

Grym settled a worried gaze on us as he put cups of tea on the table a few minutes later. "How long has it been since you two ate?"

We frowned, looked at the frog-shaped clock, and then shrugged.

"A long time," I finally got out after swallowing my last bite of breakfast sandwich.

Grym reached for a donut, going still as Sebille growled.

They had a predator to boulder man moment, until I put a stop to it.

I smacked Sebille's hand. "He brought all this stuff for us. Don't be an animal."

She narrowed her eyes on him but finally went back to eating.

Grym snagged the donut quickly and took an exaggerated step backward, making us laugh again. "So what's the game plan?" he asked after swallowing his first bite.

I expelled air and took a bracing sip of tea before launching into all my issues.

He listened carefully, nodding, and remained quiet until I told him about Rogers. His handsome face hardened. "I know that guy. He's a little crazy. He's been known to target supernormals for no apparent reason."

I didn't like the sound of that. "Does he usually get away with it?"

"Let me deal with Rogers," Grym said. "What's your plan with this ghost witch?"

"What *about* me?" a voice I hadn't expected asked behind us.

Sebille and I turned to find Rustin standing just inside the connecting door, Mr. Slimy squatting at his feet. He was frowning. "Why would you need a plan for me?"

I had a face/palm moment. Rustin didn't know what I'd learned in the vault. With a guilty glance at Grym, who couldn't see or hear the ghost witch, I explained. "Not you. Margot." I quickly filled Rustin in, his eyes growing wider and wider with every word I spoke.

"You mean she's like me?"

"Who are you talking to?" Grym asked.

I looked at Rustin and he nodded. "It's Rustin. He's trapped inside Mr. Slimy. Long story. Now's not the time to explain it all. But suffice it to say he's in *temporary* limbo." I added the emphasis on the word temporary for Rustin's sake, because I suspected he was starting to lose hope that he'd survive his limbo.

"I'm not sure if she's exactly like you," I told him. "She's basically a spirit without a body. You're a spirit in the wrong body. That makes you a pretty close fit, I guess."

"But what about the fact that she looks like you?" Grym asked, taking the Rustin news well. "That says doppelganger spirit to me."

I frowned. I just didn't know. We were in strange territory.

"The question is, how did she manage to come up with that spiritual form," Sebille said thoughtfully. "It's in a doppelganger's magical DNA to become its chosen subject. But a regular spirit should only be able to present as itself. She should look like Margot Quilleran."

"Or the owl," I agreed.

We sat in silence for a moment, thinking, until the bell over my door jangled. Lea came in carrying a box and a big, white bag.

Sebille and I looked at each other and grinned.

Lea's broad smile slid away as she spotted the copious debris from the breakfast we'd just consumed. "Oh. You already ate."

Grym stood up, indicating the chair for Lea. "Eating doesn't really cover what they did. Devouring, maybe? Gorging? Snarfing without any discernible breathing? There was even some growling."

I smacked him on the shoulder and he stopped talking, but there was a sparkle in his eye that told me it would be a while before he let me forget the snarf-fest he'd witnessed.

Lea settled the bag and box onto the table. "Help yourself, Detective. It doesn't sound like they let you have any of what you brought."

"I did manage to snag one donut, but I had to

keep my fingers away from Sebille's teeth," he mumbled, grabbing the box and holding it tightly against his chest. He showed Sebille his teeth and she rolled her eyes.

Lea sank into the chair he'd given her. "What a night."

We all glanced her way. "What happened?"

She shook her head. "I don't know. There were all these noises in the shop, and Hex spent half the night scratching to get out. But, when I'd go down to investigate, I'd always find something strange."

"Strange how?" I asked, frowning.

"One time there was a trail of herbs leading to the door..."

"What kind of herb?" Sebille asked.

"Sage. And then one window was open a crack, the sill covered in brown crumbs." Her brow knit together. "I had some chocolate cookies on top of the refrigerator and they were gone, the wrapper shredded." She shook her head. "Just stuff like that. And when things finally quieted down, Hex acted like she kept hearing the noises. She drove me crazy trying to get downstairs. When that failed, she parked herself in front of the bedroom window and kept vigil, meowing plaintively. She watched out that window all night, pawing at it."

"Don't you love this time of year?" I said, my voice dripping with sarcasm.

She yawned widely, glancing around. Her gaze

got caught on my compressed shelves. "It looks like you all had an interesting night too."

"That's putting it mildly," I grumped. "But I'm glad you're here."

She turned her full attention on me as I explained about Margot.

"Any ideas what we're dealing with, and how to vanquish her?"

"No. But let me give it some thought. Whatever she is, I'd believe Pansy about her not being a doppelganger. She would certainly recognize a fellow DS."

The blue warning light flared into life.

"Toxic vault breached!" the same female voice announced above the din. "Please remedy the situation ASAP."

"Gnat knees!" I exclaimed, surging to my feet. "What now?"

We all pounded through the dividing door, Grym and Lea jerking to a horrified halt as they saw the condition of the artifact library.

"Goddess save us," Lea murmured. She lifted a horrified gaze to me. "I'm so sorry for whining about a few missing cookies."

"Toxic vault breached. Please remedy the situation ASAP."

I gave her an apologetic smile and took off.

The vault door was wide open. No shimmering protective barrier gave me a sense of relief as I skidded to a stop in front of it. I turned to yell over my shoulder, "Sebille!"

"On it!"

I dove inside, my gaze locked on the tableau playing itself out in the center of the large room. The magic trap still shimmered in a column around Margot Quilleran, but she was no longer alone. There was a man standing inside the trap with her, his hands wrapped around her throat, his wispy face filled with murderous intent.

"Rustin!" I ran over and started to reach for him, remembering at the last moment not to touch the barrier. A single touch on the walls from the exterior could shut it down, releasing its prisoner.

My evil twin looked near death, blue eyes bulging and mouth open in a desperate attempt to gather air, it was all I could do not to drop the barrier and intervene.

"Rustin, stop it now!" I screamed in desperation, praying my voice could penetrate the haze of fury he was clearly operating under.

"She helped him do this to me," Rustin ground out, his handsome face taut with rage. "She dies today."

Clearly, it had been a mistake to reveal Margot's wispy status to Rustin. Her present state put her firmly into his universe and made her vulnerable to him in a way she never would have been in her physical form.

"Rustin!" I held my palms over the glossy magic barrier, determined to pull it down if it looked like he was going to actually kill her. "You're not like her. You're not like your uncle. You don't murder people in cold blood."

"She's stolen my life. It's only fair I should steal hers."

The bulging blue gaze slid to my hands and a speculative glint filled them. The first niggle of suspicion eased through the fear. I narrowed my eyes on Margot. That was when I saw it. The edges of her persona shifted, went slightly off-kilter, like the old erasure of a misdrawn line rising up behind the corrected line on paper, distorting it.

I held her bulging gaze, seeing the moment she realized I knew. At that moment, Margot's lips curved upward on a sneer and she reached for Rustin, wrapping her hands around his throat and squeezing hard.

Rustin's hands moved to hers, trying to pry her loose. It was touch and go for a moment, but he finally got her fingers away from his throat. He didn't waste any time skedaddling out of the magic trap. Rustin flew outward, his ethereal form gliding right through the barrier.

Margot tried to come through after him but the trap had been sprung for her. It wasn't going to let her out.

With a quick flash of energy, Margot Quilleran

no longer looked like me. "I almost had you," she said, the sneer hardening into a taut line.

I didn't know what to say to that. She was right. She'd almost had me. "Because I had the humanity not to want you killed? I won't be ashamed of that impulse. It's what makes us different, you and me. I'm proud that, despite the fact you're a horrible person, I couldn't face having any part in your murder."

The air on the back of my neck turned cold. Rustin floated up beside me and stopped. "It's as I suspected, she's not a DS. She's somehow learned how to mimic like a doppelganger. I'm guessing it has to do with the four-dimensional glamour Lea put on her."

Footsteps pounded up to the vault door, and I turned to look through the shimmering protective barrier. Lea and Grym stood on the other side, Lea holding her heaving stomach.

"Did the bat-hatted blood-sucking venomous snake woman get out?" my friend asked, panting.

Taking a beat to admire the depth of Lea's descriptive swearing, I finally shook my head. I left the vault, flinging keeper magic at the door. It swung closed with the sound of magical locks engaging. "No, but it was a close call."

Glancing toward Rustin, I noted how his gaze slid guiltily away, proving that what I'd seen hadn't all been an act. His rage against Margot and Jacob was visceral, hardly abated over time. It was a good thing Margot had finally come clean and driven him away.

Grym watched the vault close, fascinated. "Maybe we should put an extra guard on this door."

I thought about his suggestion. "Not a bad idea. Especially now that we know she's just a regular old wispy person and not a doppelganger."

He nodded. "I'll be happy to hold down the fort while you do what you need to do."

"You sure?"

He nodded. "It's the least I can do. You all saved my life not too long ago, remember?" His expression told me more than words how much he appreciated our efforts.

I reached out and grabbed his big hand, giving it a squeeze. "You don't owe me anything. I was being selfish. I didn't want to lose a friend."

His brows lifted. "Friend, huh?"

Something inquisitive slid across his gaze. I had no time to figure out what it meant. "Thanks for keeping an eye on her. I'm going to see if we can come up with a plan to shut her down."

We headed back to Croakies and Sebille made us all tea. Rustin stayed in the library to use the communicating mirror. He'd offered to contact his Aunt Madeline about Margot. I was anxious to hear if she had any solutions.

"Anything we come up with is conditional on

getting Hobs back," I reminded Lea and Sebille as we sat down.

Sebille nodded. Lea stared at her tea with such determination that I realized she had something to say which she knew I wouldn't like.

"What, Lea? Just spit it out."

She chewed her lower lip. "It's about the hobgoblin."

Panic clawed icy fingers into my belly. I forced myself to speak past it. "Tell me."

"If the owl ate him as you described…"

"We don't know for sure she ate him," Sebille said, frowning. "It all happened really fast. One second Hobs was there, and the next he was gone."

"Is it possible he left on his own?" I asked. "Hobgoblins can use transportive magics in times of great danger." Since Hobs had moved into Croakies, I'd been reading about the little creatures in Doctor Osvald's *Hobgoblins and other Pesky Vermin*.

Lea's expression turned hopeful. "Did you see a flash of white light? Or a halo of his form hanging in the air afterward?"

I studiously avoided Sebille's gaze, feeling her despair like a physical thing between us. "No, but there was a lot going on."

Hope fled Lea's face. She sipped her tea, dodging my gaze.

While all three of us sat there, avoiding looking at each other, my problems still hadn't been solved.

"Let's talk about Margot. Where's the safest place to put her?"

"We can't put her back into the mirrors, she'll continue to torture you," Sebille said. "And the abyss is out because of proximity to Jacob."

"We need someplace that will hold her permanently, with no danger to you or anyone else," Lea said thoughtfully.

"And maybe someplace safe from Rustin too," I added. They both looked at me in surprise. I shrugged. "It's true. He's as mad as a centipede with gout at that witch." I glanced at Sebille. "Did you see his face?"

"That was all an act, Naida." Sebille might bicker with Rustin on a fairly continual basis, but loyalty was one of her superpowers, and the ghost witch had apparently earned a spot on her protective list.

I didn't argue with her. It wouldn't solve anything. I dropped my head into my hands. "I need to get a couple of hours of sleep. My brain isn't working."

Sebille nodded. "Me too."

Lea clasped my hand, giving it a squeeze. "Let me know what I can do to help?"

I nodded, thanked her, and locked and warded the door behind her. I'd have to fix the store and open it for at least a couple of hours later in the day. I tried to keep as normal hours as I could for my human customers. But if I didn't get some sleep soon, I wasn't going to be much good for anything. And with Rogers breathing down my neck, I couldn't afford to make any more mistakes.

I climbed wearily upstairs, finding Wicked already curled up on his pillow on my bed, and fell across the covers, not even bothering to undress or burrow underneath them. I fell asleep immediately and slept deeply.

At least until the alarm sounded again in the toxic magic vault.

11

A GRYM PREDICAMENT

I sat bolt upright, sleep still clinging to my mind and gluing my eyes shut. I shoved a hand into my tangle of brown hair and climbed to my feet, finally managing to wrench my eyes open.

Mr. Wicked's furry gray back end was disappearing through the apartment door as I got my bearings.

Shaking my head, I stumbled toward the door. I really needed to put a GoGo camera on my cat to see how he kept opening all the doors.

I hit the stairs at a run and picked my way quickly through the clutter of artifacts still lying all over the floor, leaping over some and zigzagging for a better path. A moment later, I skidded to a halt in front of the vault door.

It was wide open again.

Gasping in fear at the sight of Grym crumpled

into a boneless pile on the floor, I dropped to my knees beside him. "Grym!" My hands found the wide gash at his hairline and then felt for the pulse at the side of his muscular neck.

"Is he dead?" my brutally straightforward assistant asked. Sebille shoved me gently aside as she crouched beside him, her hand resting on his broad chest.

"Just knocked out, I think." I stood up and glanced into the vault. The magic trap and its inhabitant were gone. Biting back a swear, I closed and locked the vault door. Much good as that had done me the last several times. "What is going on with this lock?"

Green light flared from Sebille's hand and Grym gasped, stirring. He rolled onto his back with a groan. "Did you get the license plate of the truck that hit me?"

"What happened, Grym?"

"I don't know. I was just standing there, playing a game of trying to figure out what each artifact does..." He frowned. "By the way, what's with the golden toilet paper roll holder?"

I grimaced. "You don't want to know."

"Yeah, I figured. It was quiet. Nothing was stirring. And then an explosion of light and power slammed into me. I flew off the ground and crashed into the vault with my head. I don't remember anything after that."

Sebille and I helped him sit up. "Good thing your head's made of rocks," I said, trying to lighten the mood.

"Gargoyle jokes. Good times."

Sebille snorted out a laugh.

"I'm guessing you don't know who did this?" I asked.

"I do," Sebille said.

When Grym and I looked at her, she frowned. "Isn't it obvious? The only ones who have the knowledge and permissions to open that vault are you, me..."

"And Rustin," I finished for her, stomach sinking. "Oh, Quilleran. What have you done?"

I connected with Madeline's home through the communicating mirror. At least, with Margot otherwise occupied, I no longer had to worry about her using doppelganger magic against me. Maude answered the summons rather than her aunt. "Hey, Naida! How's Wicked. I'll bet he's getting big." Her smile was as sweet as always. There was no tension in it. I took that to mean there wasn't an owl-shifting murderous witch standing behind her.

"Maude, is Rustin there?"

The teen frowned. "No. He hasn't been here

today. I think Aunt Maddie talked to him earlier, though. Why?"

"We have an emergency situation. I need to talk to your aunt."

Maude shook her head. "Sorry. She left about five minutes ago. You just missed her."

"Where was she going?" I barked the question out and had to stop myself, taking a deep breath and forcing a calm expression onto my face. "I'm sorry. Rustin's done something very dangerous. I really need to find him."

"Oh, no! What's he done?"

"He's broken your cousin Margot out of the trap we had her in. I think he intends to hurt her."

I watched Maude's expression turn contemplative. I assumed she was working up a defense for Rustin and started forming my response. But she surprised me.

"He couldn't have managed her on his own." Her gaze lifted to mine. "Aunt Madeline has to be helping him."

Hope sank. There was no way we could defeat both Rustin and Madeline to save Margot. The thought made me blink. When had magical imprisonment turned into a rescue mission? "That's not good news," I told her.

Maude shook her head. "No, it's not. And the reason why they're doing it is even worse news." Her shoulders slumped.

"You know why they took her?"

"I can guess. But I'm pretty sure I'm right. We've been struggling to move to the next step with Rustin's extraction from the frog. I'm sure Margot could be very helpful with that." Her gaze lifted, filled with worry. "Whether she wants to or not."

"Chorusing crickets!" How was I going to stop them?

A possibility flitted through my mind, but I immediately shoved it away. If I did what I was thinking, there'd be no turning back. Madeline would be sent to Area 51 and Rustin would be lost to me forever.

Not to mention Hobs.

I disconnected from Maude and slumped into a chair, feeling the weight of ten worlds on my shoulders.

"What are you going to do?" Grym asked.

I jumped. I'd totally forgotten he was there. "Only one possibility comes to mind."

His dark brows arched. "Will it work?"

"It should. But it's a risk. If I use this one card I'm holding, nothing will ever be the same again."

"You're asking yourself if it's worth that to save Margot Quilleran?" He watched me for a long moment, his gaze knowing.

Sighing, I shoved wearily to my feet, still not sure what I would do.

Rapid, clunky footsteps hurried up behind me. I

turned to find Sebille rushing toward me with my cell. "You left this in the store last night," she told me, her expression murderous. "I'm not your personal secretary, Naida."

Actually, as my one and only actual employee, she kind of was. But I didn't have the energy to argue. "What's wrong?"

Shaking her head, she shoved the phone at me and marched back toward the front of the shop. I made allowances for her sour mood, knowing she was just as tired and frustrated as I was. Lea's voice lifted into the air between me and the phone I held down by my side.

"Naida?" My friend sounded upset.

I took a deep breath and lifted the phone to my ear. "What's wrong?"

Fortunately, she didn't take offense at my brusque tone. I was about full up on crises at the moment.

"I'm sorry to bother you. I know you're dealing with a lot right now. But... Naida, my shop's been ransacked!"

L ea wasn't exaggerating. Herbal Remedies with Mystical Properties was a mess. All the jars that had been filled with dried herbs and flowers were on the ground. Some of them broken, others just empty. The contents of every single jar on her shelves was strewn about the floor, mixed and mangled as if someone had danced in the middle of it.

The shelves that had once been crammed with reference books were empty except for a few volumes lying on their sides. The rest of the ancient texts were on the floor with the jars, their pages bent beneath them.

"Oh, Lea," I breathed out.

"Why would somebody do this?"

Looking into her tear-filled blue gaze, my heart broke. I pulled her into a hug. "You didn't hear anything last night?"

"Not a peep."

"What about Hex?"

Lea frowned. "She must have slipped out of the apartment before I closed the door because I found her on the stairs this morning when I came down." She looked perplexed. "I could have sworn I'd brought her up with me, though. I'm losing my mind."

"You're not crazy. You probably did. I've given up on closing doors with Wicked around. I don't know how he does it, but he's really good at opening them all by himself."

Lea sighed. "Now that I know this happened last night, I'm relieved she's okay." The pretty little cat jumped up onto the glass counter and strode toward

Lea, purring loudly. She rubbed against Lea's arm and gave her owner soft eyes.

Lea took a shaky breath that was part sob as she took in the devastation. Hex tucked in closer and increased the volume of her purrs. After a moment, Lea calmed down. Sniffling loudly, she scrubbed moisture off her cheeks with the heels of her hands and got a mulish look on her face.

I almost smiled. I'd seen that look before. Lea was done wallowing. She was getting down to business. "Go," she told me, pushing me gently toward the door. "Do what you need to do. I'll deal with this."

"I can't leave you with the mess. You always help me with my disasters."

"But I don't have multiple crises to handle like you do. Go. Do what you need to do. If you have time later, maybe you can help me restock the shelves."

I had a thought and nodded. "I'll do you one better than that. Wait right here." I hurried out of the shop and over to Croakies, rushing past Sebille and Grym and into the library. I sent out my keeper magics to summon the artifact I wanted and waited as it descended toward me.

Lea was plugging a vacuum into the wall when I returned a few minutes later.

She looked up expectantly, narrowing her gaze on the object I held out to her. It didn't take her long to recognize it. "Is that...?" Her blue gaze went wide.

"Cinderella's wand," I said, nodding. "It will put everything back the way it was and then clean up." I frowned. "Just make sure we have it back by midnight. You don't want to see what happens when it goes rogue."

She laughed with delight. "Do I need to say Bibbity, Bobbity, Boo?"

My heart lighter for being able to help my friend, I giggled with her. "No. But it's fun to say if you want to."

Lea pointed the wand toward the books on the floor. "Bibbity, Bobbity, Boo!"

The books floated upward, righted themselves, and lifted to take their customary places on the shelves as if they'd never left.

Lea clapped her hands like an excited toddler and pointed it at the broken glass.

I left her cackling happily as chunks of glass, large to small, rose from the floor and reassembled themselves into jars.

"No, Hex!" Lea scolded.

I turned to see the cat still standing on the counter, whacking at the jars as they flew past on their way to the shelves.

I felt much better.

For about ten seconds. Then I remembered the task I had in front of me.

And my world turned decidedly less bright.

12

A SLUG SLURPING DAY IN THE NEIGHBORHOOD

*S*ebille was waiting for me when I got back to Croakies. Her face was carefully neutral. I took one look at her and frowned. "Now what?"

She turned to indicate a small figure standing by the connecting door. I almost swallowed my tongue. "Mr. Rogers."

Every time I said that name, I thought of the silly and harmless star of the children's show. Unfortunately, it was never a wonderful day in the neighborhood when Mr. Rogers from SDM was around.

"Miss Griffith," he bit out, disdain dripping from the two words.

"What are you doing here? I believe we agreed I'd have until the end of the year..."

He held up a small, pale hand, his goatee twitching. "I understand you have a rogue PTB?"

My eyes went wide, my mouth falling open. "How did you...?"

Grym walked out of the small alcove where we kept our tea things. His face matched his name. "I told him."

Nearly paralyzing anger transformed my muscles to rock. I turned a glare on him as Sebille reached out to touch my arm. If *she* was alarmed, my gaze must have been flashing silver. "What have you done?"

"He's done the correct thing," Rogers said. "And he's ensured that you stay on here at Croakies as Keeper of the Artifacts for the foreseeable future."

Shock sucked the rage right out of me.

Grym's expression didn't change as he offered me the cup of tea. "It's time someone else shouldered some of this, Naida. You've been taking everything on yourself. And it's not fair you should bear the brunt of it all."

His words were carefully chosen to send me a message. Grym was going to take Madeline's rage on himself.

I couldn't let him do that. I shook my head, gaining a slight softening of his dark-caramel gaze. A pleading look flashed across his face.

But I just couldn't let him throw himself onto the sword for me. I turned to Rogers. "I was coming to call you anyway. Detective Grym saved me the trouble." I avoided Grym's gaze. "We aren't absolutely sure what she's up to, but Madeline broke Margot Quilleran out of the magic trap we had her in, and I have no way of contacting her."

Rogers inclined his head. "When I heard from Detective Grym, I immediately dispatched an alert. It seems our PTB entered the Magical Universe. I've just been notified of Madeline Quilleran's location in another dimension, and the Powers That Be are tracking her down."

Rogers rubbed his hands together, clearly gleeful for the opportunity to ruin someone's day. He started toward the door. "This matter is no longer your concern, Naida keeper. Please tend to your affairs here. Your artifact library is in a horrifying state. And apparently, you have some security issues to address."

The store was quiet for a full minute after Rogers left. I stood rigidly, my teeth grinding together.

Finally, Grym broke the silence. "I was only going to speak to him about his harassment of you. When I reported the incidents in question..."

I held up a hand. "Wait. Are you telling me that you're the one who was responsible for siccing Rogers on me?"

"I had to submit the reports. It's my job, Naida..."

I held up a hand to stop him. "Please. Just leave."

Pain filled his expression but he nodded, settling the cup I'd refused to take onto the table. "I'm sorry,

Naida," he said, nodding to Sebille, and then he left, closing the door quietly behind him.

"Naida..."

I shook my head. "Rogers is right. This place is a disaster. We no longer have any role in rounding up Margot Quilleran. Let's just get to work doing what we're supposed to do."

She stared at me for another moment and then turned away, apparently deciding to let me cool down before trying to talk sense to me.

Unfortunately, the talking sense thing was a non-starter. I wasn't going to be calm enough to talk for a while.

Especially when I drenched myself with artifact energy and attempted to return my enormous shelving units to their normal state. The coming night was Halloween. It was the most chaotic magic night of the year. Normally, I'd be dreading it.

But not any longer.

I'd decided I would be taking charge of my life, as well as my role as Keeper. No more Miss Nice Naida.

I was tired of getting my teeth kicked in. It was time I did a little kicking of my own.

The energy sizzled against my nerve endings, burning me from the inside out. Rather than fight the pain of the intensive magic intrusion, I forced myself to calm and opened myself up to it. As if a switch had been thrown inside my magic core, energy flooded into me, filling every cell and spilling out to create a silvery glow above my skin.

I didn't have to look into a mirror to know my eyes were glowing silver as well. The magic was bigger than I was. It was a force beyond, yet still part of me. But, more importantly, it was mine to control.

I pulled the energy into my lungs like air and held it for a long moment, savoring its bite against my skin. Then I pictured the way Croakies was supposed to be and let the picture meld with the energy roiling at my core.

I released the magic in a long, raw breath that fled my lips in a thick ribbon of power, It swirled toward the compacted shelves and, slowly, with the expected screeching and thundering of massive weight being moved, drew them apart and shoved them into place.

While I held the energy, I repaired the damage wrought by the errant magical artifacts. I reinforced the picture window, making it stronger than it had ever been, and I sent my own warding into the entrances, burning away the special warding Madeline Quilleran had created to keep Croakies safe.

If I'd realized anything that day, it was that only I could make Croakies safe. And I'd do whatever was necessary to see that happen.

The energy still spat from my skin, too all-encompassing for me to contain it. The pain of its inhabitance was growing too much to stand. But I had one more thing to do before I let it go.

Walking with purposeful steps, I threw open the dividing door and marched into the library.

Sebille took one look at me and nodded, stepping back from the slow work of returning the artifacts to their assigned spots and locking them down.

I stood in the middle of the massive artifact library, lifted my hands, and closed my eyes.

My mind reached for the artifacts, identified each one, and then cataloged it in my thoughts. As I dropped each artifact into its rightful spot in my mind, I felt a ribbon of energy leave my fingertips and saw it flash toward the artifact in question.

One by one, in rapid succession, I returned each artifact to its place and locked it firmly down. When that was done, I sent an extra wave of energy to blanket the entire library, ensuring that nothing would move when the veil reached its thinnest point at Midnight.

I didn't realize how drained I was until I let the last of the energy ease away. My knees buckled. I fell toward the ground, the world spinning around me as I opened my eyes on a panicked cry.

Strong, skinny arms caught me as I fell, easing me down to the floor. I sat like a child, my legs stretched out in front of me. My eyes kept trying to go crossed, and I was panting hard, fighting to pull enough air into my lungs.

Sebille handed me a steaming cup of tea and a donut. I ate the donut ravenously, emptying the cup of tea in a single long gulp despite its heat.

Sebille handed me another donut, and I at that too. And another. And another. I think I finally started to feel better after the sixth donut and fourth cup of tea. My muscles were still limp and I was soaked with sweat, but I was no longer in danger of passing out.

I looked up at Sebille. "Thanks."

Her gaze flashed with speculation and something else. If I didn't know her better, I'd have thought she was proud of me. She inclined her head. "Let's get you upstairs. You have two hours before Midnight. You can rest until then."

Two hours? Wooly worm suspenders! I'd been working for hours.

I looked around in awe of what I'd accomplished. The library was back to the way it had been. No, it was better. Every artifact gleamed. And when I stood, with Sebille's help, I could feel slender tendrils of energy reaching for me from the objects arrayed across the shelves. The artifacts tested me, urged me forward, and offered comfort in my weakness.

Even more interesting, my mind had created an inventory of each and every magical object. With a quick thought, I could declare the exact location of each object. That would come in handy.

It was as if I'd formed a bond with the objects. I didn't know if that was bad or good, but it didn't feel dangerous, so I was going with it.

Sebille helped me to my bed and covered me. "I'm going out to run some errands. I'll wake you a little before Midnight so you can shower and eat something before the crazy starts."

I nodded, yawning widely. "Thanks, Sebille."

If she responded, I didn't know. I was asleep almost before I finished speaking her name.

I didn't dream. I don't think I even moved. But I awoke with a violent start that set my mind pumping.

The newfound bond I'd formed with the artifacts told me everything was intact downstairs. My quick check of the wards on the doors told me they hadn't been breached. And I didn't feel Sebille's presence in the store.

So what was bothering me? I shoved myself upright, my gaze sliding to the window overlooking the street. It was dark outside. Deep dark. The moon was high and fat in a sky peppered with dense, lead-gray clouds.

Shoving my covers back, I stood up beside the bed, groaning as pain ratcheted through my muscles. A darkness near the door filled my awareness. I spun around, energy spitting at my fingertips.

Madeline Quilleran stared at me, her tall, slender form at ease, and her long-fingered hands clasped gently in front of her. She didn't speak for a moment. When she did, her voice was filled with wonder. "You've finally accepted the mantle of Keeper."

I assumed she was referring to my new bond. "Where's Margot?"

Madeline's pretty face fell. "I'm afraid I don't know."

I felt my eyes go wide. I hadn't expected that. "Don't lie to me. The SDM is currently looking for you in the other dimensions. They'll find you soon enough. If you're honest with me now, I'll do whatever I can to help you."

She shook her head. "The SDM are fools. They won't find me." She cocked her head, observing me carefully. "Are they looking for my nephew as well?"

I flinched before I could stop myself. *Rustin*! "They don't know about him."

She nodded as if she'd expected my response. "No. They don't. Because he's dead."

The way she emphasized the word *dead* sent

painful spikes through my heart. I wanted to ask her if she'd given up, but I couldn't bring myself to do it.

"This is his last chance, Naida." Her voice was a whisper. Almost a plea. It sliced through me like a blade

"You think you can save him?"

"With Margot's help, yes."

"And she's willing to give you that help?"

Madeline's gaze held mine, giving nothing away and, in its very neutrality, confirming everything I already knew.

I closed my eyes, struggling with the hardest decision of my life. Should I do the "right" thing and help Rogers capture Margot, thereby damning Rustin to a terrible fate? Or should I save Rustin and live with the reality of what it meant to leave Margot in Madeline's hands?

It was an impossible decision.

Mr. Slimy hopped onto my foot and looked up at me. "Ribbit."

I stared into the fathomless black gaze and felt fear billowing through my chest.

You need to let him go, the frog told me.

I shook my head. "I can't."

It's his choice, Naida.

Tears burned my gaze.

"Aunt Maddie?"

Madeline and I spun to find Rustin, in all his handsome wispiness, hovering near the window.

"What have you done, nephew?" Madeline asked, her voice cold.

"What needed to be done. This won't be decided by you and me," he told his aunt. "Margot will decide her own fate."

The sound of heavy wings throbbed on the air and panic clawed up my spine. "You released her in the artifact library?"

Rustin's gaze held an apology. "This will never end until it ends," he told me with an infuriating fortune cookie logic. "In her defeat, we will win my release. If we fail to defeat her, then I'll die. It is just. It is fair. It's the only way my life will have the meaning I wish it to have."

"You're a fool!" Madeline spit out.

"Olly, olly, oxen free!" a snarly voice boomed from below. "Stop your hiding and come to me," Margot's voice was filled with as much amusement as challenge. I wondered at the type of creature who would face off against Madeline Quilleran with a laugh on her lips.

I guessed I was about to find out.

Rustin shrugged, his form growing more solid as the witching hour approached. "I'm in this state because I stuck to my own principles, Aunt Maddie. I'm proud not to be like so many of the Quillerans. You once told me the same. Are you still proud to be who you are? Will you allow personal need to squash that? I can't allow it for myself," he told her.

"And I won't be the cause of you succumbing to the dark either, Auntie."

The endearment did what nothing else could. It brought tears to Madeline's beautiful yellow eyes. She inclined her head, whether to hide the tears or in silent acquiescence, I wasn't sure.

But the determination in her gaze when she lifted her head again told me she'd accepted his challenge. "Fine. Let's go kick some tail feathers."

An ethereal Margot stood in the center of the artifact library, muscular legs spread wide, and strong arms arced at her sides. Like Rustin, the witch appeared nearly solid as Midnight approached. One large hand held something that looked like nunchuks, which pulsed with dull yellow energy.

She'd pulled her long, midnight hair back into a messy bun at the top of her head and her yellow gaze flashed with deadly intent.

Margot's ghostly face tightened as Madeline and Rustin emerged from my apartment, standing on the small landing to look down on her. "Magical tools only. No unfocused energy."

"I accept your conditions," Madeline said, inclining her head. Her hands sliced through the air around her hips to dissolve the long, black skirt she'd been wearing and replace it with form-fitting leather pants. She raised an arm, wiggling her long fingers, and energy flashed as a crossbow appeared in her hand.

Margot smiled. "I've been looking forward to this for a very long time."

Madeline's response was to take a running leap and bound over the railing, sailing toward the floor as she fired energy arrows so quickly from her bow that my eyes could barely follow the action.

Margot shifted the nunchuks and spun them at blinding speed, sending each arrow harmlessly away with the weapon. She seemed to dance on the air with a lightness that suited her ghostly form.

I realized as arrow after arrow smacked into the artifact shelves that Croakies was going to sustain too much damage if I didn't do something. With a thought, I called the Book of Pages to me, noting with surprise as I opened it, that my name had replaced the previous Keeper's in the front.

I smiled but had no time to enjoy the change. I quickly thought about the spot where I wanted the battle to be waged and, sending a blanket of keeper energy over the two combatants below and Rustin, I smacked my hand into the book and sent us all there.

13

A SOLUTION WITH A NEW PROBLEM

We landed in the lot behind Croakies. Energy flashed through the night as the two Quilleran witches battled, and I realized my solution had created a new problem. I'd brought the magic outside for non-magic humans to see.

I could fix that. Drawing on the magic archives of the library, I extracted the stored energy of the pink elephant I'd once housed at Croakies. The elephant was no longer in the library, but her magical signature was part of our catalog of available magics.

Starting at the edges of the large, empty lot, a pink shimmer rose from the rocky grass and lifted skyward, curving inward about a hundred yards from our heads and meeting in the center to create a visual distortion that hid our activity from human eyes.

I added a second element that would keep Margot from flying away, so the barrier served as both visual and physical containment.

As the dome closed, a sparkling wall of flashing lights flooded from the greenhouse and headed toward the battle. I watched as Queen Sindra's Fae encircled the battle, providing an extra measure of protection against having it spill beyond the barrier.

I relaxed slightly, knowing I'd done all I could do.

Turning to Rustin, I discovered he was gone. With a horrified gaze, I realized he'd joined the battle. I found him at the opposite end of the dome and watched in amazement as he leaped off the ground with a large club of some sort that had a spiked metal head. He looked substantial and strong, his leanly muscular form encased in similar black leather to Madeline's.

Rustin flew down on Margot with the club, smashing it toward her head as Madeline fired energy arrows at a dizzying rate.

Margot dodged to the side to avoid the club, catching a wrenching hit on one shoulder and taking one of Madeline's arrows in the other shoulder as she divided her focus.

Judging by the charred holes in her body and arms, Margot had suffered several hits. But nothing seemed to slow her down.

Similarly, Madeline sported a large, purplish

gash on the side of her neck and she seemed to be limping slightly, but she was still leaping into the air, spinning somersaults over Margot's head while raining a seemingly endless supply of magic down on the enforcer.

Rustin and Madeline's strategy seemed to be working. They were dividing Margot's energies and wearing her down.

After a particularly focused duel attack, Margot landed from an unsuccessful leaping attack and her knees buckled beneath her.

I held my breath, praying the nasty witch was finally succumbing to their magic.

Apparently believing it was over, Madeline threw the crossbow into the air and it flashed into a battle ax. She slowly approached as Margot struggled to shove back to her feet.

Behind the fallen witch, Rustin trotted forward with the deadly club raised above his head.

Just before they both reached her, Margot's head shot up, and I looked into her glowing yellow gaze, ice forming on my spine.

A wicked smile curved her hated lips. "You will all die!" She threw her arms above her head and an explosion of gilded energy burst on the air, sweeping Madeline and Rustin back and hitting me with the force of a freight train.

I left my feet and flew backward, smacking hard against the shimmering pink wall of my barrier. All around me, tiny Fae smacked the barrier and slid bonelessly toward the ground.

My heart broke. What had Rustin done? Had he released an unstoppable force into the world? How many would die because of his honorable intentions?

A horrifying screech filled the night. Massive wings pounded the sky, the sound banging against my eardrums as pressure built in my head.

I looked up through the blurriness of my gaze and saw the giant predator pounding toward me. In desperation, my fingers twitched toward Croakies, a prayer on my lips as I tried to push to my feet. I was too disoriented to stand. I fell back to the ground, curling into a fetal position as my head threatened to explode.

Massive, deadly claws, each one the length of my hand, curved around my leg and one arm and yanked me off the ground.

My throat warbled on a scream of agony as the owl hooted its victory and started to rise with my bleeding body in its grip. Hanging limply as the ground fell away from us, I forced myself to quit screaming and stretched my remaining hand toward Croakies, a thousand prayers for strength throbbing on my blood-flecked lips.

The owl hit the barrier and I knew I was out of time.

I began to struggle, drawing the owl's attention

and earning myself a new level of agony as the curved claws ripped deeper through my flesh.

Something smacked into my hand, and I clenched my fingers around it. Closing my eyes, I let the power infuse me, allowing it to pull the soothing release of icy calm through my system.

I heard the soft song of a second set of wings and words formed on my tongue. "Ye might think ye'll know, ye might think ye'll see, but Blackbeard's blade is on to thee."

I sensed SB flying nearby, his latent magical energy infusing me and giving me strength.

The owl pounded relentlessly against the barrier and its protective energies began to weaken.

"Ye scurvy blackguard won't be free, until the sword has done with thee."

The sword flashed upward, slicing through the creamy, dappled feathers covering the giant predator's belly.

The owl's call colored the air with the sound of pain and surprise, the end throbbing away to a sound almost human.

"Not done with thee," I breathed out, slashing again.

The owl thrashed in the air, spinning suddenly and ramming me hard against the barrier in an attempt to dislodge the blade.

I held fast to the deadly sword, but the owl must have decided to cut her losses. Margot unclenched her lethal claws and released me, letting me drop like a rock toward the hard ground below.

"Not done with thee," I murmured, closing my eyes as icy calm numbed me to my fate.

I flung my arm and sent the blade skyward, the proof of its lethal aim coming back to me in the burbling scream of the owl. The enormous form slipped past me on the air. A heartbeat later, I heard her smash into the rocky grass below.

I expelled a relieved sigh and let the calm consume me as I fell.

Bright, twinkling lights flashed against my lids. My downward plunge was abruptly halted. I opened my eyes to find the Fae surrounding and easing me down, their tiny wings like the sound of a hundred dragonflies in the silence.

As I landed in the rocky grass, my hand opened and the sword fell free. I hadn't even noticed when it had returned to me. A colorful flurry of feathers landed next to it. "Ye look like the victim of a murderous pirate, lass."

"Thanks, SB. That makes me feel so much better." I groaned as Blackbeard's calming magic slid away, leaving me to the harsh reality of my pain. "Goblin boogers! That hurts."

Sebille buzzed over me, hanging on the air with her hands on her tiny hips, glaring down at me. "Well, are you just going to lie there all day?"

Anger flared and my mouth opened to give her a

spitting rebuke. Then I realized it was over. Margot was gone. We were all safe. And I just didn't feel like yelling. So I started to laugh. And once I'd started, it was almost impossible to stop.

I was sitting at the table in the bookstore, staring at my order forms and seeing nothing. I'd been staring at them for over an hour, too weary and too depressed to actually do anything with the data on the carefully compiled forms.

Physically, I was fine. Sebille had healed the worst of my wounds and I was left with just a general achiness and a deep malaise, which I suspected was more depression than injury.

Sebille had tried to knock me out of my mood with her usual gruff, irritating banter but, when I just ignored her, she finally gave up in a huff and went to the library to do something.

With my extra magical lockdown, we'd come through Samhain swimmingly. All the artifacts were in place and no damage had been done to Croakies.

Yay me.

Unfortunately, I'd lost Hobs and had no idea what was going to happen with Rustin. When I'd become aware enough to ask about Margot, all Sebille had told me was that her death had been reported to the SDM and the body would be disposed of. She later assured me Madeline was no longer on SDM's rogue PTB list, and she'd been credited with Margot's capture.

By the way that Sebille's green gaze kept skating away from mine as she informed me of Madeline's reprieve, I assumed one Detective Wise Grym had probably had something to do with that.

Sebille had been right about Margot's body. It *had* disappeared. Really quickly in fact. And nobody in the surrounding area had seemed unduly alarmed by all the magical activity so my pink elephant barrier must have worked.

But...I'd still lost Hobs and maybe Rustin. I hadn't seen him since the night before. I had no idea if the ghost witch was still driving the Slimy bus. The fat amphibian refused to talk to me. I was trying not to take that as a bad sign. If Rustin was gone-gone. Then I wasn't sure if the frog would be *able* to talk.

The thought made me dizzy with fear, and my head hit the notebook in front of me.

Everything was horrible.

I was a terrible person.

The least I should be able to do was protect my friends. Yet, somehow, I was never able to do that.

Dragon's fiery garlic breath. I totally and completely sucked.

"Naida?"

My instinctive reaction was to snarl at the intruder to go away and leave me alone. Then my mind glommed onto the fact that it wasn't Sebille. I looked up as my friend Lea walked through the door, Cinderella's wand in her hand and a careful smile on her pretty round face. "I brought this back. Sorry, I'm late. More stuff happened last night and I needed to use it again this morning."

All I could dredge up by way of a response was a silent nod.

Her smile dimmed. "Are you okay?"

I started to tell her I was fine, but the words wouldn't come. Instead some tears came. Lots and lots of tears, until I was afraid I might flood the hapless order forms with them. "No," I said. "I've lost Hobs and I've probably lost Rustin and I'm sure Grym's mad at me and I'm definitely mad at him and..." I took a breath and noticed Lea's smile had widened.

I narrowed my gaze on her. "And you look like you're happy about it."

My accusation failed to wipe the smile from her face. She bit her bottom lip. "Last night, several pictures fell off the wall in my shop. Hex's bowl was turned over, and the fresh herbs and flowers were dumped all over the floor..."

I frowned. "Lea, I'm sorry..."

She held up a hand. "Let me finish, please. I was

sitting in the shop when it all happened. I was stunned. It looked as if somebody or something was flailing around trying to...I don't know, get somewhere else, maybe? But I had no idea what could be causing the disturbance. Then I caught a tiny glimpse, and I thought I knew. Fortunately, I had a frosted chocolate donut that I'd saved from this morning and..."

Hope flared. "A chocolate donut?"

She nodded, bouncing excitedly on her toes. The door behind her opened. A tiny creature with a dirty blonde shock of hair between oversized ears stepped inside. "Hello, Miss."

I erupted from my chair with a squeal. Hobs blinked his large blue eyes in alarm, diving behind Lea for protection.

I hurried over and dropped to my knees, opening my arms to pull him into a hug. He let me hug him for a long moment and then pulled back, tears sliding down his cheeks. "I was lost, Miss. I couldn't find my way back."

I looked at Lea. She was nodding. "I think he blipped himself away when Margot attacked and inadvertently entered a different layer in this dimension. I'm guessing, in that other layer, *my* shop was part of Croakies, maybe the artifact library. In a panic, he would have gone there because that's his safe zone." She shook her head as if all that wasn't important. "Anyway, I had this spell that I started working on after you and Wicked went into the Universe and visited that other Croakies..." Seeing my attention fading as I stared at Hobs, Lea wiggled her hands. "Long story short, I opened an inter-dimensional door and there he was!"

I sniffled, my tears happy for once. I grabbed the little guy into another hug. "I'm just so glad to have you back."

Hobs let me hug him again and then pulled away, erasing my tears with a soft fingertip. "No more crying, Miss. Hobs is home."

I laughed, nodding. "You should go tell Sebille. She's been really worried about you."

He nodded enthusiastically. "Thanks, Miss."

Grinning widely, the little guy ran toward the dividing door. Turning to give me a thumbs-up, Hobs reached for the handle...

The door slammed open before he could turn it...

And it hit him right in the face, sending him sliding across the carpet to smash against my knees.

Sebille stood in the door. "I thought I heard..." Her green gaze found Hobs and her eyes went wide. "Oh. Oops. Did I do that?"

"Sebille," I said, scolding. "You need to be more careful." I reached a hand toward the hobgoblin. "Are you okay...?"

But my fingers never found him.

Hobs jumped off the ground, his blue eyes sparkling with pleasure as he screamed Sebille's favorite word. "Again!"

And I watched Sebille's face light up like a Christmas tree.

READ MORE ENCHANTING INQUIRIES

Did you enjoy **Croakies & Scream**? If so, you might want to check out Book 6 of the *Enchanting Inquiries Paranormal Mystery series*.

Please enjoy Chapter One of **Frosted Croakies**, my gift to you!

'Tis the season for great folly...walawalawalawalala... ribbit.

It's Christmas time at Croakies. The tree is up. The stockings are hung. And Christmas tunes are turning the atmosphere jolly. After a tumultuous Samhain, I've found my chi again and I'm starting to enjoy the season of love and giving.

Yeah. You probably know how this is going to end.

When Sebille suggests I open the bookstore up to a small holiday party, I foolishly agree. How was I supposed to know that the hobgoblin would decide it would be fun to hide everybody's stuff? Or that we'd be hit with a freak winter storm that confined everybody inside for the duration. Or that a "You're me but who am I?" spell would be released inside the shop, switching everybody's identities and creating general chaos and hysteria?

I could probably deal with all that if it weren't for the fact that my friend, Lea...the one person who could possibly reverse the spell...was ensconced in SB the parrot, with no opposable thumbs for spelling.

And me? Of course, I'm sitting fat and squishy inside Mr. Slimy. Thank goodness Rustin isn't currently in residence, or it would be really crowded in here.

Who spelled my party? What do a pair of Santa's elves have to do with it? And why have old enemies suddenly become new friends? I apparently have a little holiday mystery to solve inside Croakies, and I have no idea how I'm going to solve it with everybody mixed up and some of us human.

Have I told you I hate this season?

Ribbit!

FROSTED CROAKIES

"I definitely need to get my head examined," I groused under my breath.

Passing by carrying a box filled with ornaments, Sebille reached up and flicked me on the temple.

"Ow!"

She narrowed her eyes menacingly. "Stop complaining. It's going to be fun. It's about giving back to your customers. Some of them have been coming to Croakies for years, and they're very loyal."

She was right. I was being a Scrooge. I thought of Mrs. Foxladle and Mr. Peabody, two of my favorite customers. They were the kindest souls in the world, and I did enjoy the idea of thanking them for their loyalty and support over the years.

I tugged the last branch of the artificial tree straight and stepped back, squinting at it with a critical eye. "Does that look crooked to you?"

From his perch on the windowsill, looking out into a snowy Saturday afternoon in December, Mr. Wicked gave me his expert, feline opinion. "Meow."

"Thanks, buddy," I told him.

Sebille straightened up from her box of goodies and gave the tree the once-over. "It looks perfect."

There was a soft rustling noise and I turned back to the tree as Sebille hurried away, saying something about lights. The tree was leaning at least six inches to the right.

"Sebille must need glasses," I said, reaching through the branches and tugging it straight. I jammed the whole thing deeper into the stand and infused it with a wisp of magic to keep it there.

I straightened with a groan and stepped back to get a better view.

"Ribbit," Slimy said from his glass tank.

I glanced his way. "I think it's finally straight, don't you?"

Another soft rustling sound had me whipping back around.

The top third of the tree sagged slowly downward, like a Charlie Brown Christmas tree.

Suspicion flared. "Okay, who's messing with me?"

Giggling ensued from somewhere inside the tree. I hurried around back to catch the culprit, and Hobs flew out of the tree, shooting away from me so quickly he left only a streak of color on the air from the red and white holiday scarf he'd taken to wearing around his neck.

Wicked jumped down from the sill and plodded after his friend.

I should have known. The two of them were inseparable. Where there was a Wicked, there was always a hobgoblin.

Sebille settled another box on the floor. "I think that's it." She looked at the tree, frowning. "You broke it."

I sighed. "It wasn't me, it was Hobs."

"Oh." She grinned.

I was really glad she was enjoying the hobgoblin's antics. I was about ready to put a lump of coal in his stocking. The only thing stopping me was that I feared he'd eat it.

I reached up and tried to straighten the top portion of the tree, but I wasn't tall enough. I struggled for a minute, blowing prickly needles off my face as I strained on the very tips of my tippy toes. I huffed out a frustrated sigh as I failed to seat the section properly back into its center support.

"Here, let me try," Sebille said. She popped into her Sprite form on a burst of white light and fluttered upward, her multi-hued wings beating the air behind her as she sent a soft green glow to bathe the sagging treetop in energy. Prodded by a gentle spurt of magic, the sagging segment surged upward and dropped firmly into the center pipe.

I wiped my sweaty palms onto my jeans. "Thanks, Sebille."

She nodded and pointed to the lights. "Give me the end of that, and I'll attach it to the top."

With her flying around and around the tree, we had the lights in place within only a few minutes. I gave her the lighted angel I'd purchased for the top. She put that into place before she popped back to full size again.

My day was looking better. The hard part was done. "Now, all we need to do is add the ornaments," I told her with a smile.

The front doorbell jingled behind me. I turned around to find Lea and Hex blowing in on a blast of icy air. Lea had her head so deep into her frothy, cream-colored scarf she resembled a turtle trying to retreat into her shell. The lumpy brown coat only enhanced the image. The scarf was ginormous, seemingly wide and long enough to serve as a blanket on a twin-sized bed.

My friend smiled brightly at me as Hex hurried toward the back room, gray tail whipping the air with excitement. "It's not fit for man nor beast out there," she said poetically.

Lea handed me something wrapped in foil that smelled like cinnamon and pumpkin. "Merry almost Christmas."

I took the weighty gift and pulled her into a hug.

A snowflake sifted from her scarf and melted on my nose. "Merry almost Christmas, Lea."

Sebille plugged the lights in and our tree exploded with pulsating color and light.

Lea sighed. "So pretty."

Christmas music suddenly filled the air. I squinted at Sebille. "Did you do that?"

She shook her head.

"It was me, Miss."

Hobs stood near the door between the bookstore and the artifact library, his long-fingered hands clutching a small box inexpertly wrapped in red and green plaid foil with a crooked green bow on top. "I brought you a present."

His oversized, pointed ears twitched with embarrassment and his pale cheeks pinkened.

"That's so sweet," I told him, walking over to retrieve the box from his spidery fingers. "Should I open it now?"

He shook his head. "It's your Christmas spirit, Miss. You must keep it intact until the exact moment when you lose hope for the season."

I wasn't sure what to say to that. It was kind of a mixed message. I finally settled on the obvious question. "What if I don't need to unwrap it?"

His grin made him look positively angelic. Good thing I knew better. "All the better, Miss."

I held the box up to my ears. The music was coming from inside. It sounded like an entire orchestra, the sound amazing. "This is wonderful, Hobs. Where did you get it?"

He held up a chastising finger, rocking it back and forth in censure. "Uh, uh, uh, Miss. Don't look a gift spirit in the mouth."

Or...something like that.

I gave him a hug. "I'll put it under the tree." I took a couple of steps toward the tree and stopped, despair making my skin prickle. "We forgot to get a tree skirt!" I immediately regretted the whiny tone of my voice, but I had no time to go back out and get a skirt. Especially since the stores were ridiculously busy and a little scary at that time of year.

"Here, Naida." Lea came to my rescue. Unwinding the enormous scarf, she dropped to her knees beside the tree and wrapped it carefully around the stand. The result was beautiful.

Tears burned my eyes. "Oh, Lea. Are you sure?"

"Absolutely. I came to help you get ready. I'm glad I could solve that one problem, at least."

I gave her another hug and then settled the box onto the scarf. It looked perfect nestled there. I considered the foil-wrapped delicacy in my other hand and decided against leaving that there. When I looked at Lea, it was like she'd read my mind.

"I agree. Between the cats and the hobgoblin, that wouldn't make it through the day."

"We'll slice it up and serve it at the party," I said,

loving the idea. Then I had a thought. "You, um, didn't put anything extra in this, did you?"

Lea's eyes sparkled. "Maybe."

"There will be humans here."

"It's okay. It won't hurt them. Think of it as catnip for people."

I laughed. "As long as it doesn't make them climb the drapes."

A box of pretty red and green glass bulbs appeared in front of my face. Sebille's not-so-subtle reminder that we had a tree to decorate.

"What do you want me to do?" Lea asked, tugging off her coat.

"Can you get the big table from the back, find the tablecloth for it, and start arranging the food?"

She nodded briskly and took off toward the artifact library. I turned to the tree with my load of bulbs. With a slightly fizzy stomach that told me I was still worried about the evening to come, I set to work placing ornaments on the tree. Smiling and singing along with the music throbbing through the room with the force of a full orchestra, I felt my holiday spirit start to rise.

———

Check out the entire series here: https://samcheever.com/books/#enchanting

ALSO BY SAM CHEEVER

If you enjoyed **Croakies & Scream**, you might also enjoy these other fun mystery series by Sam. To find out more, visit the **BOOKS** page at www.samcheever.com:

Reluctant Familiar Paranormal Mysteries
Yesterday's Paranormal Mysteries
Gainfully Employed Mysteries
Silver Hills Cozy Mysteries
Country Cousin Mysteries

ABOUT THE AUTHOR

USA Today and WSJ Bestselling Author Sam Cheever writes contemporary and paranormal mystery and suspense, creating stories that draw you in and keep you eagerly turning pages. Known for writing great characters, snappy dialogue, and unique and exhilarating stories, Sam is the award-winning author of 80+ books.

To learn more about Sam and her work, visit her at one of her online hotspots:
www.samcheever.com
samcheever@samcheever.com